"How about some help? What do you need?"

"Adam, you've already helped me more than anybody in town."

Lauren hadn't consciously realized just how much until she said it out loud. "I'm sure you have your own work to do."

"Not so much that I can't spare a few hours."

"I wouldn't feel right—"

He held up a hand. "You're not going to win this argument, so you might as well put me to work."

She lifted an eyebrow. "And here everyone has been telling me you're a nice guy, but you've got a bossy streak."

He smiled, and she tried to pretend she hadn't felt a flutter in her middle.

Lauren gave up.

And if she admitted the truth, she liked having him around. With each interaction, she was beginning to believe more and more that everyone who said he was a genuinely nice guy was telling the truth.

As long as she didn't allow herself to admire him *too* much...

Dear Reader,

One of the many cool things about being a writer is that I get to live vicariously through my characters. I can experience the time-honored task of rounding up cattle on a ranch, the thrill of riding in a rodeo under the arena lights or, in the case of Lauren Shayne, the heroine of *Twins for the Rancher*, being an awesome cook and TV personality. (FYI, in real life I'm not either of those things.)

My hope is that when you read about the residents of Blue Falls, you not only feel as if you're experiencing their lives, but also find yourself rooting for them to find their happily-ever-after.

Thanks for all your support of and love for Blue Falls, Texas.

Trish Milburn

TWINS FOR THE RANCHER

TRISH MILBURN

HARLEQUIN® WESTERN ROMANCE

Recycling programs
for this product may
not exist in your area.

ISBN-13: 978-1-335-69958-9

Twins for the Rancher

Copyright © 2018 by Trish Milburn

Printed in U.S.A.

Trish Milburn writes contemporary romance for the Harlequin Western Romance line. She's a two-time Golden Heart® Award winner, a fan of walks in the woods and road trips, and a big geek girl, including being a dedicated Whovian and Browncoat. And from her earliest memories, she's been a fan of Westerns, be they historical or contemporary. There's nothing quite like a cowboy hero.

Books by Trish Milburn

Harlequin Western Romance

Blue Falls, Texas

Her Perfect Cowboy
Having the Cowboy's Baby
Marrying the Cowboy
The Doctor's Cowboy
Her Cowboy Groom
The Heart of a Cowboy
Home on the Ranch
A Rancher to Love
The Cowboy Takes a Wife
In the Rancher's Arms
The Rancher's Surprise Baby
Her Texas Rodeo Cowboy

Visit the Author Profile page at Harlequin.com for more titles.

Thanks to Beth Pattillo for helping me brainstorm
Lauren's character and for being a friend
from back when I was taking my first fledgling
steps into the world of romance writing.

Chapter One

The floorboards creaked as Lauren Shayne took her first steps into the building that she'd become the owner of only minutes before. Her hands shook from the enormity of what she'd done. The mortgage on what had been a German restaurant called Otto's years ago wasn't small, but neither was her dream for the place.

A dream that she would have never guessed would take her so far from home.

Despite her initial "this is perfect" reaction to seeing the inside, the fact it was four hours from her home in North Texas gave her significant pause. Taking the leap had required a week of denial, then pondering and number-crunching after every adult member of her family had told her to go for it. She'd finally reasoned she could get the place opened and leave the day-to-day running to a manager who lived in Blue Falls or nearby. If it did well enough for her to expand in the future, then maybe she could finally find a space closer to home.

But she couldn't let her imagination run wild. Not when there was still a lot of work and a ton of luck standing between her and making even one restaurant a success. Loyal watchers of *The Brazos Baker* cooking show, or fans of her cookbooks and magazine alone, weren't going to be enough to keep the place afloat. And she needed to get the bulk of the work done before her TV show resumed production after the current hiatus—that would require her to be back in her kitchen on a regular basis.

She attempted a deep breath, but it was a bit shaky. She hoped she hadn't just gambled her daughters' future security away with a bad business decision.

As her steps echoed in the rafters, where forgotten cloth banners decorated with German coats of arms hung, Lauren saw beyond the dust and detritus to a restaurant filled with people enjoying her grandfather's prize-winning barbecue, and baked goods made with her recipes, while they took in an unbeatable view of Blue Falls Lake.

She smiled as she imagined the look on Papa Ed's face when she finally revealed the finished product to match the images that had been in her head for a couple of years. At times, those images and the support of her family had been the only things that got her through one of the toughest periods of her life.

"Now, that looks like the smile of a woman about to do great things."

Lauren startled at the sound of a guy's voice and grabbed the back of a dust-covered chair at the sight of a tall man standing between her and the front door. He held up his hands, palms out.

"Sorry, I didn't mean to scare you."

"Can I help you?" Miraculously, her voice didn't reveal the runaway beating of her heart.

"Actually, I'm hoping I can help you." He didn't advance any closer, giving Lauren a few moments to take in his appearance, looking for clues to his meaning.

Dressed in dark slacks, pressed white shirt and pale blue tie, he didn't come across as a laborer looking for a job. She guessed he stood a bit over six feet, had sandy brown hair and was attractive in that clean-cut "businessman who used to be the high-school quarterback" sort of way.

"Tim Wainwright with Carrington Beef. We provide top-quality beef products to restaurants all over Texas. And it's an educated guess that a barbecue restaurant is going to need a lot of ribs and brisket."

Lauren tilted her head slightly. "How could you possibly know I'd be here or that I planned to open a restaurant? I literally signed the papers fifteen minutes ago."

Tim smiled. "I'm just that good."

Lauren made a sound of disbelief. This guy was full of himself.

Tim motioned, as if waving off his previous words. "It's my job to know when potential new customers come on the scene. I heard from a friend on the local city council about your plans and that you were closing on the property this morning. Took a chance we'd cross paths."

"You must really need the business if you're here now." She indicated their surroundings, covered with enough dust they could probably make dust castles. "As you can see, I'm a long way from opening my doors for business."

"It's never too early to make a good decision."

She lifted an eyebrow. Did he brainstorm these business pickup lines? Her thoughts must have shown on her face because the teasing look on his disappeared. He reached into his pocket and retrieved a business card, which he extended as he walked closer.

"I'd like to sit down with you when it's convenient and discuss what we can offer you. Dinner tonight, perhaps?"

There was something in the way he looked at her that made her wonder if his invitation was just about business. Or did he use his good looks to his professional advantage? That thought did not sit well with her. And with good reason.

"I'm afraid I won't have time tonight." Or any night, she thought as she accepted his card. "But when I'm ready to make those kinds of decisions, I'll know how to reach you."

She thought for a moment he might press for the "hard sell" approach, but thankfully he just nodded.

"The dinner invitation is a standing one. I'm through this area quite often."

She simply nodded and offered a polite smile. No need to reveal that when she wasn't working on *Brazos Baker*–related business, she was doing her best to not suck at being a mom. She'd save that tidbit in reserve in case he attempted to get personal. Nothing like the responsibility of twins in diapers to scare off unwanted advances.

Evidently getting the message that he wasn't going to make any more progress today—professionally or otherwise—Tim gave a nod of his own and headed for the exit. Halfway there, he turned and took a few steps backward as he scanned what would become the dining room.

"Can't wait to see what you do with the place."

After he left, she was hit with just how much work she faced before decisions such as which food vendors to use made any sense. And none of that work was going to move to the "completed" column if she didn't get to it. She rolled up her sleeves and took another step toward her dream.

IT WAS TIME for Adam Hartley to stop stewing over the potential customer he'd lost and forge ahead. His family had been understanding of the time and funds he'd put in to the branded-beef operation so far, but each day he wondered when that understanding would disappear. Everything his siblings did in addition to their regular ranch duties added to the Rocking Horse Ranch's bottom line. Sure, Sloane's camps for underprivileged kids cost money, but those funds were now coming from the product endorsements her new husband, Jason, had signed after winning the national title in steer wrestling the previous winter.

Adam kept reminding himself that big rewards required big risks. He just hoped his risks ended in the types of rewards he envisioned.

At the sound of the front door opening, followed by fast-approaching footsteps, he looked up from the list of possible customers throughout the Hill Country and into Austin.

"I have great news," Angel said as she darn near slid into the dining room like Tom Cruise in *Risky Business*.

"You sold some photos?" His sister was slowly gaining recognition for her beautiful photos of ranch and rodeo life.

"No, great news for you."

He leaned back in his chair. "I could use some of that."

"I just heard from Justine Ware that the Brazos Baker is opening a restaurant here in town."

"Who?"

"The Brazos Baker, Lauren Shayne." At what must be a confused look on his face, she continued, "She has a cooking show on TV. Mom watches it all the time. She has a magazine, too. Some cookbooks. And now she's planning to open a barbecue restaurant in what used to be Otto's."

No, anywhere but there.

Part of him was excited to have such a high-profile prospective customer, but he'd had his eye on that building for a while. His imagination had seen it as a mercantile filled with Rocking Horse Ranch–branded products—prime steaks from their herd, Ben's hand-tooled saddles and leatherwork, Angel's photographs, his mom's chocolate cake. He'd seen it all so clearly—except for the money to make it possible. The branded-beef operation was supposed to fund those big ideas, but he needed time for it to grow. Time he evidently no longer had.

He had to stop investing so much time and energy in the cart before he could even afford the horse. But maybe, despite the disappointment, this opportunity would help him take a leap forward toward the eventual goal. A goal that would now have to reside somewhere else, though at the moment he couldn't imagine where.

Still, the prospect of supplying not only a restaurant of that size, but also one operated by someone famous felt like Christmas presents for the next decade dropped into his lap.

Angel motioned for him to stand. "You need to go shower and put on clean clothes."

"Um, why?"

"Because when I came through town just now, I saw

vehicles at the restaurant. She's probably there right now, just waiting to hear all about awesome locally grown beef."

A shot of adrenaline raced through him. When he started to gather the papers strewn across the table, Angel waved him away.

"I'll take care of this. Go on." As he headed toward the bathroom, Angel called out, "Oh, and tell her Mom loves her show. Maybe that will win you brownie points."

Adam raced through his shower and getting dressed. Before hurtling out the door, however, he decided he should learn a little bit more about this famous cook before showing up to meet her unprepared. He couldn't blow his only shot to make a positive first impression. He opened his laptop, which Angel had deposited in his room, and did a search for the Brazos Baker.

A quick web search brought up her page. He wasn't prepared for the beautiful, smiling face that greeted him. With that long, straight blond hair and those pretty blue eyes, she looked one part model and one part girl-next-door. He wasn't a viewer of cooking shows, but he had to admit the deep-dish apple pie in her hands made his mouth water.

He forced himself to navigate away from her photo and read about how she got her start—learning from her grandmother, entering 4-H baking competitions, publishing her first cookbook when she was only twenty. Lauren Shayne appeared to be a lot more than just a pretty face.

Nowhere on her site was there any mention of plans for a restaurant, but perhaps that was under wraps. Well, it would be until the Blue Falls gossips got hold of the news, which they probably had ten seconds before she'd even rolled into town. The fact his sister had already found out and blown in like a storm to tell him was proof enough of that.

Not wanting to delay contacting her any longer, he shut down his computer and headed out the door. As he drove toward town, he couldn't keep his imagination from wondering what it would mean to have his family's beef used by a celebrity. Would she mention it on her national television program? The possibilities began to supplant some of the disappointment over her choice of building.

His mind skipped ahead to Rocking Horse Ranch beef appearing on the menus of fancy hotels and the catered events of the increasing number of actors and musicians calling the Austin area home. A flash of brown on the side of the road intruded on his daydream a moment before a deer jumped in front of his truck.

He hit the brakes and tensed less than a breath before the unavoidable *thunk* and jolt as he hit the deer dead-center. His heart was still racing when the hiss of steam rose from his radiator. There were times when Adam thought his family's motto should be One Step Forward, Two Steps Back. Why did that deer decide today was the day he couldn't handle the pressures of life anymore and taken a flying leap in front of a pickup truck? A truck Adam had bought used and finally managed to pay off exactly one week ago, just in time for its tenth birthday. And as a bonus, it appeared his air bags were not operational.

After turning on his hazard flashers, he stepped out onto the pavement to verify the deer that had gotten knocked into the ditch was indeed dead. One look was all the confirmation he needed. Same with the front grille of his truck. With a sigh, he pulled out his phone and dialed Greg Bozeman and his always-busy tow truck.

Half an hour later, instead of introducing himself to Lauren Shayne and singing the praises of his family's locally raised beef, he was at Greg's garage, waiting for the man to tell him how much the tow and repairs were going to cost him.

He considered buying a bag of chips from the wire rack to calm his growling stomach, but he figured that was a buck he should save.

Greg stepped through the doorway between the repair bays and the small office of the garage, which had been in his family for as long as Adam could remember.

"I think your family could keep me in business just replacing radiators and front grilles."

Adam knew Greg was referring to when Adam's brother Ben had accidentally run into Mandy Richardson's car the previous year thanks to a pigeon flying through his truck's window and hitting him in the side of the head. He'd had to repair Mandy's car, but it hadn't turned out so badly in the end. Ben and Mandy were now happily married with an adorable little girl. Adam was pretty sure his encounter wasn't going to turn out with that sort of happily-ever-after ending. The best he could hope for was the lowest possible repair bill Greg could manage.

"Yeah, seems the area wildlife has it in for us."

"At least the deer didn't hit you in the head."

After Greg gave Adam the estimated price and said he needed a couple of days to complete the repairs, he asked if Adam needed a ride anywhere.

"No, thanks. Got a couple things to take care of in town." He'd figure out how to get back to the ranch after that.

Greg waved as he picked up his ringing phone.

Adam started walking toward downtown Blue Falls, thankful the day was overcast so he wouldn't be sweating buckets by the time he reached his destination. Now he needed Lauren Shayne's business more than ever. He'd launched the branded-beef business with his family's blessing, hoping to contribute his part to the diversification that would allow the Rocking Horse Ranch to stay solvent and in the family, something that had been touch-and-go on more than one occasion. But if he didn't land some big accounts soon, he wasn't sure how much longer he could keep seeing money going out without enough coming back in.

Sure, the business was less than a year old, but there wasn't a day that went by when he wasn't conscious of the figures in the operation's balance sheet. None of his siblings, or his parents, had said anything about his shuttering the operation, but he was also aware that his attempt to carve out a distinctive place for himself in the family's business was costing more than Ben's saddle-making or Angel's photography supplies.

By the time he reached the restaurant, he'd managed to adjust his attitude from his earlier annoyance to being the friendly, approachable local businessman he needed to be to meet a potential customer. A small blue hatchback sat alone outside the building. He grinned at the big yellow smiley face sticker on the hatch. It was surrounded by several other stickers—a few flowers, one that said I Brake for Cake, one of a stick figure lying beneath a palm tree and another that read Don't Worry, Be Happy.

Lauren Shayne seemed to be a happy-with-life type of person. He supposed that was easier when your business was a roaring success. Although her car didn't look as if it was driven by one of the rich and famous.

Well, if nothing else, maybe some of her happy vibes would rub off on him and finish vanquishing his frustration and concern.

He took a deep breath, stood tall, fixed his pitch in his mind and walked through the large, wooden double doors. The first thing he saw when he stepped inside was Lauren Shayne standing on the top step of a ten-foot ladder, stretching to reach a banner hanging from one of the large posts supporting the ceiling. His instinct was to steady the ladder, but he was afraid any sudden movement would cause her to fall. Instead, he stood perfectly still until she gave up with a sound of frustration and settled into a safer position on the ladder.

"Would you like some help with that?"

She startled a bit, but not enough to send her careening off her perch, thank goodness.

"Can I help you?" she asked.

He couldn't help but smile. "I thought that's what I was offering." He pointed at the banner.

She stared at him for a moment before descending the ladder. "That's not necessary. I'll get some help in here at some point."

"I don't mind," he said as he walked slowly toward the ladder, giving her ample time to move away. His mom had taught him and his brothers to never make a woman feel as if she was trapped or threatened. The fact that there was only one vehicle outside and no signs of other people in the building told him that Lauren was here alone. "You almost had it anyway. My just being a little taller should do the trick."

She didn't object again so he climbed the ladder and nabbed the cloth banner bearing some unknown German coat of arms and several years' worth of dust. When his feet hit the wooden floor again, he held up the banner.

"This thing has seen better days."

Lauren made a small sound of amusement. "That it has."

He shifted his gaze to her and momentarily forgot what planet he was on. The picture on Lauren's website didn't do her justice.

"I'd introduce myself, but I'm guessing you already know who I am." She didn't sound snotty or full of herself, more like...

"I suppose you've already had several visitors stop by."

"You suppose correctly."

"Small town. News travels fast."

"Oh, I know. I grew up in a town not much bigger than Blue Falls."

He found himself wanting to ask her about where she grew up, to compare experiences of small-town life, but his visit had a purpose. And that purpose wasn't to keep Lauren talking so that he could continue to appreciate how pretty she was or how much he liked the sound of her voice, which for some reason reminded him of a field of sunflowers.

Wouldn't his brothers—heck, even his sisters—hurt themselves laughing over the thoughts traipsing through his head right now?

"So, the question remains, what brings you by?"

Right, back to business.

"I'm Adam Hartley, and I wanted to talk to you about locally sourced beef from the Rocking Horse Ranch."

"No mistaking this for anything but the heart of Texas. You're the second beef producer to come see me in the last hour."

Someone had beaten him here? He silently cursed that deer for making him later to arrive than he planned. A sick feeling settled in his stomach.

"May I ask who it was?"

Please don't say Carrington Beef. They'd claimed a number of contracts he'd been in the running for, and if he missed out on being first with this huge opportunity because of hitting a deer, he might have to go to the middle of the ranch so he could scream as loud as he was able.

"Carrington Beef."

Somehow Adam managed not to curse out loud, though the parade of words racing through his head was certainly colorful.

Lauren pulled a business card from her pocket. "A rep named Tim Wainwright."

It was as if Fate said, "You think I can't make your day any worse? Here, hold my beer."

Chapter Two

"Honestly, it's going to be a while before I'm ready for any sort of food products," Lauren said as she shoved the business card back in her pocket. She lifted her gaze to Adam Hartley's in time to see a flash of what looked like frustration on his face before he managed to hide it.

"I understand," he said, back to the friendly, engaging man he'd been since his arrival, as if the moment when he'd clenched his jaw and then finally let out a breath had been nothing more than a figment of her imagination. "I'd appreciate it if I could tell you about our products, however."

His approach was different enough from Tim Wainwright's that she wanted to give him a chance. It was possible that his good looks—dark wavy hair, lean build and a face that was far from difficult to look at—might be a factor in her decision, too. She wasn't interested in getting involved to any extent with anyone—might never be again after what Phil had put her through—but it didn't hurt anything to look.

And while Tim Wainwright had also been attractive, his personality was a little too slick and polished—a bit too much like Phil's, she now realized—for him to appeal to her in that way. Granted, it could all be an act he put on for work, but it didn't really matter. She was so not in the market for a man. The market wasn't even on the same continent.

"If you don't mind talking while I work, go for it."

"Okay," he replied, sounding a bit surprised by her response.

"I'm sorry. I don't mean to be rude. It's just that I have limited time to get a lot done, and I'm running behind." Which hadn't been helped by all the interruptions. Well-meaning ones, but interruptions nonetheless.

"No need to explain. I should have called ahead and made an appointment to meet with you."

"Hard to do when you don't know the number."

"True." He smiled, and wow, did he have a nice smile. He ought to be able to sell beef to half of Texas on that smile alone.

But she also knew better than to trust smiles alone. Phil had an attractive smile, too—until you realized it belonged to a snake.

"The Rocking Horse Ranch has been in my family nearly a century. Everyone who works there is family, and we have a history of producing high-quality beef products—steaks, ground, ribs."

As she listened to Adam's sales pitch, she grabbed one of the tables she aimed to get rid of and started dragging it toward the front wall.

"Here, let me help you with that." Adam lifted the opposite side of the table and together they carried it away from the middle of the large dining room.

Before she could voice an objection to his continuing to help her with manual labor, Adam launched back into his spiel.

"I'm sure you already know that diners are more and

more interested in where their food comes from, and with our products you'd be able to tell them it's from a few miles down the road, raised by a family that's been part of Blue Falls for a hundred years."

She had to give him credit—he certainly was passionate about his family's business. Considering her own strong ties to family and the hard work to share her love of food with others, she admired that passion. Still, when it came down to the decision-making, it would have to be based on the price and quality of the beef. Adam Hartley could have all the charm and belief in his products the world had to offer, but it wouldn't matter if she didn't deem his ranch's beef good enough to associate with her own brand.

"Sounds as if you have a fine operation," she said. "If you'll leave your card, I'll call for a sample when I'm closer to making those types of decisions."

After a slight hesitation, he nodded and retrieved a card from his wallet, then handed it over. The ranch brand was like none she'd ever seen before, a little rocking horse like a child might use. She made a mental note to provide rocking horses for the girls when they were old enough.

"Interesting brand."

"With an interesting story behind it," he said as he helped her move another table.

"Well, don't keep me hanging."

"Shortly after my great-grandfather bought the first part of the ranch acreage, he found out my great-grandmother was pregnant with their first child, my grandfather. He used part of a tree he cleared where the house was to be built to make a rocking horse for the baby. And he made the first sign with the name of the ranch using what was left."

"That's sweet."

"Yeah, my mom gets teary every time she tells that story. Oh, by the way, I was informed by my sister to tell you that our mom is a big fan of your show."

"I appreciate that. Are you a fan?" For some reason, she couldn't resist the teasing question.

He placed one of the old chairs next to the growing collection of furniture she needed to get out of the way. "I'm just going to be honest here and say that before today I didn't even know who you were."

She caught the look of concern on his face, as if maybe he'd just shot a giant hole in his chances to land her business. Even seeing that, she couldn't help but laugh.

"I can't say that I'm surprised. I wouldn't peg you as the main demographic."

"If it helps, I do like baked goods. I don't think I've ever said no to pie, cake or cookies."

She pointed at him. "And that's what keeps me in business, the country's collective sweet tooth."

Without direction, Adam rolled an old salad bar toward the rest of the castoffs. "I hope you don't mind me asking, but if you're known for baking—"

"Why a barbecue restaurant?"

"Yeah."

"My grandfather has won more blue ribbons than I can count in barbecue competitions. I want to feature his recipe. He's actually the reason I'm here." She gestured toward their surroundings, glancing up at the high ceiling with the log beams that she imagined gleaming after a good cleaning and polish. "He grew up in Blue Falls."

"I wonder if my parents know him."

"Probably not. He left about fifty years ago."

"Has he moved back?"

She shook her head. Not unless you counted the fact he was camped out at their hotel babysitting while she worked.

"No, and yet he somehow convinced me that this was the place to launch the next phase of my business."

"Blue Falls is a good place to settle."

"I won't be living here, either," she said. "I'll just be here to get this place up and running, then I'll leave it in a manager's hands and go back home."

"Which is where?"

That felt a little too personal to reveal to a man she'd just met.

"Sorry, didn't mean to pry."

Settling for a compromise answer, she said, "North Texas."

Lauren realized when they picked up the next table to move it that it was the last one. "So, have you been helping me haul all this stuff in the hopes I'll award you a contract?"

"No, ma'am. Just being neighborly."

He seemed genuine with that answer, but she wasn't sure she totally bought it. Or maybe she was just extra cautious now, having been so recently burned in a very public way. She wondered if Adam Hartley knew about that. She found herself hoping not, and hated the idea that her recent troubles were what sprang to mind when people saw her now. Maybe if he hadn't known who she was before today, he didn't know all the ugly backstory, either. That would be refreshing.

"Okay, neighbor, I could use a suggestion of who to call to make all this stuff disappear." She pointed toward the pile of furniture they'd moved. It was still serviceable but not at all like what she had in mind for her restaurant.

"Actually, I know someone who would probably love to take if off your hands at no cost. She repurposes things other people don't want anymore."

"Sounds great."

He pulled out his phone and started scrolling through his contacts until he found what he was looking for, then extended the phone to her. She added Ella Bryant's name and number to her own phone before returning his to him.

"Well, I best get out of your hair," he said as he slid the phone back into his pocket.

"Are you kidding? You helped me make up for all the time I lost this morning."

"Glad to help, ma'am."

"Lauren, please."

"It was nice talking with you, Lauren. I look forward to hearing from you about that sample."

As he walked toward the front door, she thought that if she was any other single woman who'd had any other recent past than the one that she'd just experienced over the past eighteen months, she might want a sample all right. A sampling of Adam Hartley.

ADAM HURRIED ACROSS the parking lot of what had until this morning been his dream purchase. Well, he supposed it was still technically a dream, but one that wasn't going to come true. But maybe he could still salvage something positive from the unexpected turn of events. Though he didn't have any sort of commitment of her business, he thought the meeting with Lauren had gone pretty well. He'd even managed not to allow his instant attraction to her show. At least he hoped it hadn't. Now he just needed to get out of sight of the restaurant before she noticed he'd arrived on foot. It wouldn't speak to his professionalism and the success of his company that he didn't even have a running vehicle to drive.

Thinking about his damaged truck brought to mind the fact that he'd almost beaten Tim Wainwright to the punch this time. It was as if the man had spies all over Central Texas, feeding him advance information about potential customers. Judging by the number of accounts Adam had lost to the man, he'd wager Wainwright's commission income was quite a tidy sum. Enough to make him cocky. The times they'd crossed paths, Wainwright acted friendly but it was in that way that said without words that he knew he was always going to win the day. He really hadn't changed that much since his days as quarterback at Jones-Bennett High, one of Blue Falls High's biggest rivals.

Adam's jaw tensed just thinking about the guy's smug look if Carrington Beef convinced Lauren to go with their products. That commission alone would probably send Wainwright on some Caribbean vacation. He likely didn't have a family ranch he was trying to take to the next level, to save for future generations. The idea of Lauren doing business with him stuck in Adam's craw.

Though their initial meeting had gone well, Adam felt as if he needed to do something more to bring Lauren over to his side. But he couldn't be pushy, wouldn't put on a practiced smile and say whatever necessary to garner her business. There had to be a happy medium. He just had to figure out what that was, and quickly.

His stomach let out a growl that would make a grizzly jealous. Thankfully the sound had held off until he was out of earshot of Lauren. Before he texted some member of his family for a ride home, he aimed to settle the ravenous beast. Lunch at the Primrose Café would be a perfect solution. Maybe while he downed the daily special, some tremendous idea for guaranteeing Lauren went with Rocking Horse Ranch beef would occur to him.

At the sound of an approaching vehicle, he moved farther onto the side of the road. When the car slowed and stopped next to him, he looked over and saw Lauren staring back at him. She looked confused, probably because she hadn't passed any disabled vehicles between her building and him.

"Need a ride?"

"I'm good, thanks."

As if to negate his words, a rumble of thunder picked that moment to accompany the overcast skies.

"I wouldn't be very neighborly if I let you get drenched, would I?"

With a sigh, he opened the passenger-side door and slipped inside the car just as the first raindrops fell.

"Thanks."

"No problem. Where to?" Thank goodness she didn't ask him why he'd been hoofing it down the shoulder of the road.

"Primrose Café, downtown."

"They have good food?"

"Yeah."

"Great. I'll give it a try, too. Was headed out in search of lunch, just hadn't decided where. Though I look a fright."

"No, you don't." Far from it. "And besides, the Primrose isn't fancy. You'll see everyone from tourists to ranchers who have a load of cattle waiting outside."

When they reached the café, the parking lot was pretty full. With her small car, however, she was able to squeeze into a space that would hold only about half of his truck if he split it down the center. Thankfully, the spot was close to the door.

"One of the joys of having a small car," she said. "Along with great gas mileage."

They raced for the front door to the café, which he held open for her.

"Thanks." She offered a brief smile, but it was enough to make his insides feel wobbly. He looked away, trying to convince himself it was just his hunger reasserting itself.

Lauren got the attention of a waitress when they stepped inside. "Who do I see about placing a to-go order?"

"Any of us. But honestly, you'll probably get your food faster if you just eat here. We got a big group take-out order in about two minutes ago, so you'd be behind all those. Different cook working on dine-ins."

Adam looked around the crowded room, not unusual for this time of day, and spotted a two-top over by the wall. He caught Lauren's gaze and pointed toward the table. "You're welcome to join me if you think you can stand me a little longer."

He tried not to take it personally when she hesitated a little too long before nodding.

They'd barely sat down before a woman at the next table said, "Oh, my God. You're the Brazos Baker, aren't you?"

Lauren smiled, similar to the smile she showed on her website. It was different than the more natural ones she wore when not in what could be considered the public spotlight.

"Yes, ma'am."

"I don't believe it." The woman looked at her friends, who suddenly appeared just as excited. "We all love your show."

"I made your pineapple cream cake for my daughter's wedding," one of the other women said. "I had to hide the top tier for her and her husband or it would have been gobbled up, too."

"Well, I'm glad everyone enjoyed it."

The back-and-forth was interrupted by the same waitress who'd greeted them at the entrance. "What can I get for you?"

They hadn't even cracked the menus open, not that Adam ever had to. Other than the daily specials, the menu at the Primrose didn't really change. Still, Lauren hadn't been here before.

"She needs time to look at the menu," he said.

"No, I'm okay. You go ahead. I can decide quickly." She opened up her menu to give it a quick perusal.

"Burger and fries for me," he said, not feeling the daily special of turkey and dressing.

"That actually sounds good," Lauren said. "Give me that, too."

When the waitress hurried away, Lauren pulled out her buzzing phone. "Sorry, I have to respond to this."

"No need to apologize. You're a busy woman."

She flew through answering the text like a teenager who could text faster than she could speak. He took the opportunity to text Angel for a ride home after he ate. When he looked up, Lauren pointed at his phone.

"Looks as if I'm not the only one."

"Arranging the family version of Uber." At the curious expression on her face, he confessed, "I might have run over a deer and crunched the front of my truck on the way into town."

"Oh, no. My sister once completely destroyed her car when she hit, I swear, the biggest buck I've ever seen. He was like a ninety-eight-pointer or something."

He laughed at that mental image. "Bet he had a neck ache before his untimely demise."

One of those genuine smiles appeared on her face, and he swore he'd never seen anything so beautiful.

The waitress had been right. She appeared with their food just as the other staff members behind the counter started bagging up a large number of takeout containers. As their waitress moved on to her next customers, he noticed a couple of the women who'd been chatting with Lauren were now looking at him. They smiled then shifted their gazes away, but he felt odd, as if they'd been sizing him up.

He'd taken one bite of his burger when the group of women started making moves to leave. When they stood, the one who'd originally recognized Lauren drew her attention again.

"I'm so glad to see you doing well and moving on. The way that boy treated you was so wrong. I wanted to hit him upside the head with my purse, and it's not an unsubstantial weapon," she said, lifting what to Adam's eyes looked more like a piece of luggage.

"Uh, thank you." Lauren's answer sounded strangled, as if she suddenly wished she was anywhere but where she sat.

Thankfully, the women didn't stick around any longer, especially since one of the waitresses was already clearing their table so more customers could be seated. But Adam only saw that activity with his peripheral vision because his gaze was fixed on Lauren and how any hint of a smile, of happiness, had just evaporated right before his eyes.

Chapter Three

Lauren had read books where the characters were placed in situations so embarrassing that they wished for a hole to open up and swallow them, but she'd never experienced it herself. Not until now anyway. Even during the trial Phil had forced her into with claims she'd promised him half her business, she hadn't experienced the need to pull herself into a shell to hide like a turtle. Then she'd had her attorney beside her, and she'd been filled instead with righteous anger and a fierce determination to prove that Phil was full of crap and not entitled to one red cent of her money.

The determination had paid off. Only after it was all over did she realize the emotional toll it had taken on her. But as the woman had said, Lauren was moving forward—just not in the way the other woman had assumed. Before Lauren figured out some way to correct her while also not offending Adam, the woman and her friends were already headed for the exit.

Oh, how she wished she hadn't gotten a text from Papa Ed earlier that he and the girls had already eaten and were about to take a nap. She'd intended to order her lunch to go so she could head back to work. She wanted to get a good amount accomplished but also leave plenty of time to play with Bethany and Harper before their bedtime.

Movement across the table brought her back to the present. She couldn't meet Adam's gaze, didn't want to invite any questions about what the other woman had meant. Hoping by some miracle he'd missed it entirely, she latched on to the first nonrelated topic that came to mind.

"So, you said your company only employs family members. How many people is that?"

"We're up to eleven if you don't count the kids, although one's a toddler so she gets a free pass." She smiled at his joke, causing him to do the same. "Some have other jobs, too, but we all pitch in on the ranch whenever and wherever needed. You're welcome to come out and see the operation sometime, if that would help make your decision easier."

"I'll keep that in mind," she said, more out of gratitude that he'd not asked about the woman's comment than any real need to see the beef still on the hoof.

Thankfully, their conversation flowed into even safer territory with him telling her about the various businesses in town that brought in tourists, or that were popular with the locals—or both.

"You're going to have some competition from Keri Teague. She owns Mehlerhaus Bakery and is considered the best baker in Blue Falls."

"I don't mind a little friendly competition. It's been my experience that there can never be too many desserts available. The number of people with a fondness for sweets is directly proportional to the number of sweets they can get their hands on."

Adam laughed. "You and Keri should get a cut of Dr. Brown's business. He's the local dentist."

She smiled. "That's not a half-bad idea."

Adam's smile lessened a fraction as he glanced beyond her. Before she could turn to investigate why, an older woman stepped up to the table and placed her hand on Adam's shoulder.

"I hear your family's about to get a little bigger again."

"You hear correctly."

Was Adam married? She didn't see a ring on his hand, but that didn't mean anything. She knew ranchers who didn't wear rings so they didn't get caught on machinery and rip off a finger. Of course, he could be a father without a wife. He had mentioned kids on the ranch earlier. Though she barely knew him, she really didn't want to believe he might be married and having a friendly, chatty lunch with her. She was well aware that men and women had business lunches all the time, but the fact that Adam didn't come across as a married man made her hope he wasn't. Not that she wanted to be with him. She just didn't want to be faced with another lying, self-serving man.

Adam made eye contact with Lauren. "My oldest brother, Neil, and his wife just announced they're having their first baby."

"Oh, good for them." She ignored the strange and unexpected feeling of relief that the child wasn't his. She tried finding a valid reason for her reaction. When she couldn't, she chose to ignore it.

"Yeah, it's so nice seeing all the joyful events your family has been having—weddings, babies." The woman shifted her attention toward Lauren. "I'm sorry. I must have left my manners in the car. I'm Verona

Charles. I wanted to welcome you to Blue Falls. Everyone is so excited to have you here, and we can't wait to see what you do with your place."

"Thank you. I appreciate that." She wondered if there was a soul left in the county who didn't know what she was up to. She accepted Verona's hand for a shake. "It's nice to meet you."

"Verona used to be the head of the Blue Falls Tourist Bureau before she retired," Adam said.

"Yeah, but old habits die hard. I still have this urge to greet newcomers and visitors as soon as they cross the city limits."

Lauren caught a shift in Adam's expression—as if he was trying really hard not to smile or maybe even laugh. What was that about?

"Verona, your order's ready," one of the waitresses called out from behind the counter.

"Oh, I better get that. Taking lunch out to everyone at the nursery."

After Verona took her leave, Adam explained her final statement. "Her niece, Elissa, owns Paradise Garden Nursery, a big garden center a short distance outside of town. That's another tourist draw to the area, especially in the spring."

"Ah. So now explain what was so funny."

"You caught that, huh?"

She nodded as she swirled a fry through her pool of ketchup.

"I guess someone should warn you. Verona has appointed herself town matchmaker. If you spend any time here at all, she'll try to pair you up with someone."

A cold ball of dread formed in Lauren's middle. A matchmaker was the absolute last thing she needed in her life right now.

ADAM CONSIDERED HIMSELF lucky that his attempt to not laugh at Verona was all Lauren had noticed. If she'd guessed that he'd momentarily been okay with the idea of Verona trying to match up the two of them, that likely would have been the end of any chance he had of winning her business. He had all the evidence he needed in her reactions to what both the unknown woman and Verona had said. He wasn't Sherlock Holmes or anything, but even he was able to deduce she wasn't interested in a romantic relationship. He had to admit he was curious why, but he wasn't about to ask such a personal question of someone he'd met only a little more than an hour ago.

After they'd finished their meals, he asked Lauren if she wanted dessert.

"Better not. I'm so full now that I'm likely to want to take a nap when I get back instead of working."

"Speaking of, you'll want to be careful with that ladder, especially if you're alone. When I first came by earlier, I was afraid you were about to topple off it."

"I'll be careful. A full body cast isn't my idea of a good time."

"That's nobody's idea of a good time."

After they both paid for their meals, he once again held the door open for her. The rain had passed, leaving behind a faint hint of sun trying to burn its way through the clouds.

"You need a ride somewhere else?"

He spotted Angel just pulling into the parking lot. "No, thank you. My ride just showed up."

She glanced across the parking lot. He could tell when she spotted Angel.

"One of the family members who works at Rocking Horse Ranch?"

He nodded. "My sister, Angel. She's mainly a photographer, a darn good one, but she's been known to string fence and muck out stalls."

"My little sister dabbles in photography, too. Nature stuff, mostly. Does Angel specialize?"

"Ranch life and rodeos. She's beginning to gain some recognition, has had some photos in a couple of national magazines."

"That's great. Well, I'll stop talking your ear off and let you get on with your day."

"No problem. Hope to hear from you soon."

She simply nodded and headed toward her car, and he hoped he hadn't come across as too pushy. He didn't think he had, but you never knew how far was too far for other people.

When he realized he'd been watching her a bit too long, he turned away and headed for Angel's vehicle.

"That was her, wasn't it?" Angel asked as soon as he opened the door to her car.

"Yeah."

"Looks as if things must have gone well if you two had lunch together."

"I think our meeting went okay, but lunch was just an accident."

Angel started the engine but didn't pull out of the lot. Instead, she watched as Lauren drove by and gave a quick wave to them.

"How does an accidental lunch happen exactly?"

With a sigh, he recounted the story of his morning, right up until Lauren had given him a ride to the Primrose.

"Well, that's a good sign."

"Not necessarily. She was just being a decent person, preventing me from getting soaked to the bone."

"I'd give you that except she agreed to have lunch with you, too."

"It wasn't her first choice." As Angel finally drove out of the lot onto Main Street, he told her how he and Lauren had come to share a table.

"She could have waited for takeout or gone somewhere else."

"Yeah, but she was hungry then."

"Whatever. I just think you must have made a good impression."

He hoped so, and he tried to tell himself it was only for professional reasons.

"I think she's already in Verona's crosshairs."

"I wonder who Verona has in mind for her," Angel said, not even trying to disguise her teasing tone.

"Well, judging by Lauren's reaction to the idea of a matchmaker, I'm guessing Verona is out of luck on this one."

"Oh, I suppose that does make sense."

"What does that mean?"

"Lauren went through a really ugly and public breakup with her fiancé. And then the bastard took her to court, tried to sue her for a big chunk of her profits."

"Did he help her start her business or something?"

"No. From what I read, he claimed she'd promised him a half stake when they got married. When the engagement got called off, he sued, saying he was still entitled to what he was promised."

"He sounds like an ass." Adam supposed this ex could have been cheated somehow, but his gut told him Lauren wasn't the type of person who would treat someone that way. He based that on the look he'd seen on her face when the woman at the café had mentioned the guy doing Lauren wrong. She'd seemed very adamant in her support of Lauren. What was it with men who couldn't treat women decently?

"That's the general consensus," Angel said.

"Verona ought to know about that and lay off."

"Maybe she thinks the way to get past such a bad breakup is to find someone new and better."

"She might mean well, but she should mind her own business."

"I've wondered sometimes if Verona is lonely. She's never married, and I've never seen her out with anyone."

"Still doesn't give her the right to push people together."

"I think it's more like gentle nudges."

Adam snorted. "I'd hate to receive one of those nudges if I was anywhere near a cliff."

When they reached the ranch, he changed back into work clothes so he could help his brothers replace some rotting timbers on the side of the barn. As he rounded the corner of the barn, he spotted Neil first. His eldest brother was standing back and watching as Ben nailed a board in place.

"Playing supervisor again?" Adam asked.

Neil smiled. "Perk of being the oldest."

"Yeah, you're going to feel old soon when that baby gets here," Ben said. "I speak from experience. There were days in those early months after Cassie was born that I almost had to tape my eyes open to get any work done."

Suddenly, Adam felt more separate from his brothers than he ever had before. Their lives had moved into a different stage, which included marriage and children. They could share experiences, along with their sister, Sloane, to which he had nothing to add. Even Angel had a child, though no husband. In that moment, Adam felt more like an outsider than he had since arriving on this ranch as a child.

"How'd the meeting go?" Neil asked, drawing Adam's attention back to something they did have in common— the ranch and its long-term viability.

"Pretty good. Will be a while before anything can come from it, though."

"Just make sure you kick Wainwright's butt this time," Ben said.

Adam decided not to reveal that Wainwright had beaten him to Lauren's door. He had to believe that one of these days the Rocking Horse operation was going to triumph over Carrington. And he admitted to himself that there was another reason he hoped he would win the contract with Lauren. It would be no hardship to see her on a regular basis. Or would it? He was attracted to her, but he respected that the feeling wasn't mutual. It would have to be enough if they had a business relationship, maybe even became friends.

But as he helped Ben and Neil finish making the repairs to the barn, he couldn't manage to push Lauren from his thoughts. He considered how Neil, Ben and Sloane had all found their other halves when they were least expecting it. And tried not to think about how he sure hadn't expected his reaction to Lauren Shayne.

LAUREN WALKED OUTSIDE the restaurant with two cold bottles of water in hand to find Ella Bryant and her husband, Austin, loading the last of the tables onto a trailer hooked up to their pickup.

"You two look thirsty," Lauren said as she extended the bottles toward them.

"I feel as if I could drink the lake," Austin said as he hopped down from the trailer.

"Eww," Ella said.

Lauren laughed. "Pretty does not equal potable."

Austin did manage to drink half the contents of his bottle before coming up for air, however.

"I really appreciate all this," Ella said.

"Thank Adam Hartley. He's the one who suggested I call you."

"I'll do that. He's a good guy. All the Hartleys are good people."

"That's reassuring to hear about someone I might do business with in the future."

"I haven't had their beef," Austin said, "but that family is as honest as anyone you'd ever hope to meet."

Now that was more welcome to hear than they could possibly know. Honesty was pretty much at the top of her list of desirable traits these days.

Lauren pointed toward the load of discarded furniture. "I have to admit I'm curious to see what you do with all that."

"I have more ideas and materials now than I have time to implement. But I guess that's a good problem to have."

"It is indeed."

Ella nodded toward the building. "Do you know what style you're going to put in its place?"

"Honestly, it's going to be like picking the building—I'll know it when I see it. But I want it to be Texas-themed. Part of the building is going to be a store filled with items with that theme, as well."

"You should check out the antiques stores in Poppy. They've always got neat stuff, lots of big items that could be turned into unique tables, large metal Texas stars. And there are a lot of craftsmen and artists in the area who I'm sure would be interested in putting their items in your store if that's the way you want to go with it. We have a local arts-and-crafts trail, so you could surreptitiously check them out in advance if you wanted to."

Now that did sound promising. "Thanks for the tip. I'll do that whenever I get the chance."

"Well, we'll let you get back to work," Austin said. "We look forward to your opening."

"Thanks." She waved goodbye to them, then went back inside to tackle washing all the windows. She'd been putting it off for three days because she hated the task so much. It probably made sense to just wait until all the interior work was done, but she wanted a better idea of how the place would look at different points of the day through actual clean windows. How the sun hit would likely influence how she organized the dining room and the shop.

But the moment she stepped inside, the enormity of the job—not to mention the time she'd have to spend on the ladder Adam had warned her about—hit her, and she just couldn't face the task today. In truth, she didn't feel as if she could face much more than a hot shower, dinner and a face-plant into her bed at the Wildflower Inn.

But mommy duties awaited, and the thought of seeing her smiling babies gave her a boost of energy. At least two wonderful things had come from her relationship with Phil.

She promised herself she'd tackle the windows tomorrow, then grabbed her keys to lock up. As she drove the short distance to the inn, her thoughts wandered through the names and faces she'd met since her arrival in Blue Falls. Everyone seemed nice and she could see why Papa Ed had fond memories of the place. Though she'd been hesitant initially about placing her flagship restaurant here, now she could see that it would fit in perfectly with the community's other offerings.

Thankfully, no one else had mentioned Phil or the trial, so they either didn't know about it or had decided not to bring up the topic. She'd prefer the former but would take either. What she wanted more than anything was to forget Phil even existed and that she'd ever been so blind that she hadn't seen through to his real motive for wanting to marry her. She would never make that kind of mistake again.

For some reason, she wondered if Adam Hartley now knew all the details. After meeting him and Tim Wainwright, she'd done an internet search on both their companies. So it would stand to reason they'd done the same for her. She felt sick to her stomach thinking about Adam sitting in front of his computer reading about the trial. He seemed like a nice guy, but she detested the idea that someone learning about her past might see her as an easy mark.

She shook her head, not wanting to be so cynical. Instead, she'd rather think of Adam as a potential friend. She didn't want him to know about what Phil had done, because it might taint the possibility of a friendship without the accompanying pity she'd seen in the eyes of more than one person she knew. Their hearts were in the right place, but those reactions had only served to make her feel like an even bigger fool.

When she reached the inn, she didn't immediately get out of her car. Instead, she sat in the quiet, looking out across Blue Falls Lake, its surface painted gold by the slant of the setting sun. This area was pretty now, even with winter approaching. She'd bet it was gorgeous in the spring, when all the wildflowers were blooming and carpeting the roadsides throughout the Hill Country.

Hopefully, all the busloads of tourists who visited the area in search of the iconic bluebonnets would fill her restaurant to bursting and keep the cash registers busy. Maybe it was petty or needy of her, but she wanted her first venture since leaving Phil to be so successful he choked on the idea of all the money not going into his pockets. And it would provide undeniable proof that his claim she would be a failure without him was complete garbage.

Not wanting to think about her ex anymore, she made her way inside.

She heard the girls giggling before she even opened the door to her room. When she stepped inside, she smiled at the sight that greeted her. Papa Ed was playing peekaboo with Bethany and Harper, much to their mutual delight.

He straightened from where he was sitting on the edge of the bed next to the girls' travel crib. "Look who's home," he said in that special voice he used with his great-granddaughters.

Lauren didn't point out that nice as it was, the Wildflower Inn wasn't home. Instead, she headed straight for her little blonde bundles of grins and baby claps. She lifted Bethany from the crib and booped her nose with the tip of her finger.

"Have you been good for Papa Ed today?"

"They were angels, of course," Papa Ed said as he picked up Harper and delivered her into Lauren's other arm.

"I think Papa Ed is fibbing, don't you?" she asked Harper, drawing a slobbery smile.

"Well, you can't fault them for being fussy when they're cutting teeth."

"Yeah, probably a good thing that's something none of us remember doing." Lauren sank onto the chair in the corner of the room so the girls could use her as a jungle gym. "So, what did you all do today?"

"Before the rain, we went for a stroll through the park and played in the sandbox they have down there," he said, referencing the public park at the bottom of the hill below the inn. "We had a picnic and watched ducks on the lake."

"That sounds like quite the exciting day." She dropped kisses on the top of both her babies' heads. "You must be worn out," she said to her grandfather.

"Not at all. We had a nice nap this afternoon. Plus, reinforcements are on the way. Your mom called and said she was coming down to see the new place."

Lauren laughed a little. "I think it's more likely she's coming to see these two."

"Can't say that I blame her. She's never been away from her grandbabies this long."

"My girls are going to be spoiled so rotten they'll stink all the way to Oklahoma."

"There is no such thing as too much spoiling."

Lauren outright snorted at that comment, making the girls startle then giggle at the strange sound Mommy made.

"I'm pretty sure that's a recent change in opinion. I don't recall it being in place when Violet and I were growing up."

"When someone becomes a great-grandpa, he's allowed to change his mind."

Lauren smiled and shook her head.

"How did your day go?" he asked.

She gave him the rundown as well as what she hoped to get accomplished tomorrow.

"I wish you had some help."

"I will eventually. I just need to be conscious of my expenses right now and do everything I can myself. Plus, Violet will be here soon. She's almost caught up with everything on the to-do list that needs to get done before she can work remotely."

"I'm so glad you two work so well together," Papa Ed said.

"I don't know what I'd do without her, especially over the past year and a half. But don't tell her that or she'll get a big head."

Papa Ed chuckled. "You're probably ready for a shower."

"That I am. And then some food."

He took Harper from her just as there was a knock on the door. Lauren carried Bethany with her as she went to open it. Her mother's face lit up as soon as she saw Bethany. She immediately held out her hands for her granddaughter.

"Gammy's here," her mom said, resulting in some excited bouncing by Bethany.

"Well, I see I've been usurped," Lauren said as she handed over her daughter.

"Someday you'll enjoy being the usurper when they have babies of their own."

"A long, long, long time from now." She was barely used to the idea of having two children of her own. There wasn't enough room in her mind to even contemplate grandchildren someday.

Once the girls were safely ensconced with her mom and grandfather, Lauren grabbed clean clothes and headed for the shower.

After washing away another day of dust and sweat, she was surprised by how much better she felt. She came out of the bathroom to find a note saying for her to join her family in the dining room. When she arrived, she found them talking with Skyler Bradshaw, the owner of the inn.

"Good evening," Skyler said. "I couldn't resist stopping to see these little cuties."

Harper held Skyler's finger as if she'd known her from the day of her birth.

Lauren gently caressed the pair of downy heads. "They do have the ability to stop people in their tracks."

"Is there anything I can do to make your stay more pleasant?"

"No, thank you. Everything has been wonderful."

"Glad to hear it."

After Skyler moved on to chat with other guests, Lauren slipped onto her seat and pulled two jars of baby food from the diaper bag decorated with baby animals.

"Do you want to see the building after dinner?" she asked her mom.

"No, tomorrow's soon enough. Tonight, I just want to spend time with my granddaughters."

Bethany let out an enthusiastic squeal as if to say that was the best idea ever, drawing chuckles from the older couple at the next table.

"Nice set of lungs on that one," the older guy said.

"Let me assure you they are twins in every way," Lauren said as she held a tiny spoon of green beans up to Harper's lips.

After they'd all had a delicious meal, Lauren accompanied her mom back to the room they would share while Papa Ed headed back to his own for a well-deserved rest and, if he could find one, probably a fishing show on TV.

Once back in her room, Lauren opened her computer to check if there were any pressing messages. She grinned at the sight of her mom tickling the girls' bellies, making them laugh.

"They adore you."

"The feeling is mutual." Her mom glanced toward Lauren. "Are we interrupting your work?"

Lauren shook her head. "I've had about enough work for the day. Just checking email and social media."

"If you want to go to sleep—"

"No. It's too early. If I went to sleep now, I'd wake up at two in the morning."

Despite having worked all day, an odd restlessness took hold of her.

"You should go out and do something fun."

"I've already left the girls with Papa Ed all day. I can't just pass them off to you now."

"Why not? You never take time for yourself."

"There's a bit too much on my plate for spur-of-the-moment girls' nights. Besides, I barely know anyone here."

Despite her protestations that she shouldn't just up and leave the girls again after being gone all day, Lauren couldn't concentrate on anything. Maybe it was that she felt confined in such a small space.

Or maybe her mom was right. Since her breakup with Phil and the discovery not long after that she was pregnant with not just one baby, but two, Lauren hadn't taken any real "me" time. She told herself she couldn't afford it, or it wasn't right to leave the girls or expect her family to take care of them while she went off to do something that wasn't work-related. And now she'd added opening a restaurant to the mix, as if she had an unending reserve of both time and energy.

"Why don't you at least go take a walk?" her mom said. "It's supposed to be a lovely, clear night, not too cold yet."

This time Lauren didn't argue against the idea. "I won't be gone long."

"No need to hurry back. These little stinkers and I will be right here discussing all the yummy things their mommy will bake for them when they have more teeth."

The mention of teeth caused Lauren to remember Adam Hartley's comment about her getting a share of the local dentist's profits. A ball of warmth formed in her chest at the memory of how easy it had been to talk with him, even after the awkward moment with the other woman at the café.

"Lauren?"

"Huh?"

"You had this faraway smile on your face." The unspoken question in her mom's tone sent a jolt through Lauren.

"Just imagining how I'm going to convince the daughters of a baker that they can't have dessert for the main course of every meal."

After a couple minutes of loving on her babies, Lauren left the room for an evening stroll to clear her head and stretch her legs.

Though there was a slight chill in the air, she decided on a walk through town. She felt like meandering along Main Street, since it was quieter and less crowded than during the middle of the day.

As she checked out the window displays of the downtown shops, she made a mental note to do some Christmas shopping soon. It'd be much easier to keep her purchases secret if she shopped when her family was otherwise occupied, especially Violet. Her sister had a habit of trying to find and figure out what her presents were well before Christmas morning. The habit was so annoying that their mother had threatened to stop buying her presents on more than one occasion. Violet would swear she'd reform, but that only lasted about a day at most. Lauren thought Violet perhaps did it mostly to see everyone's reaction.

She promised herself she'd check out the cute outfit displayed in the window at Yesterwear Boutique, see if A Good Yarn had the lavender-scented candles her mom liked and browse the shelves at the little bookstore. At some point, she'd introduce herself to Keri Teague, the resident baker of Blue Falls, and hope Keri didn't see her as an adversary. But though the bakery still appeared to be open, Lauren didn't feel up to it tonight.

As she eyed a lovely western-themed living room set

in the window of a furniture store, the sound of music drew her attention. She followed it to what turned out to be the Blue Falls Music Hall. A man in cowboy attire opened the door for a woman, allowing the sound of a band playing to rush out into the early evening. She found herself walking toward the entrance. After all, if she was going to be a local business owner, she should support the other businesses in town. Maybe it would help pave the way into the fabric of the town, toward acceptance, considering she was an outsider.

She knew how small towns worked. While she had a recognizable name that could bring in additional tourists, some locals might see her as unfair competition. Her goal was to assure everyone she wanted to create a mutually beneficial relationship with the lifelong residents of Blue Falls. She'd only stay a few minutes then return to the inn.

The moment she stepped into the building, Blue Falls didn't seem so small. That or the entire population of the town had crammed inside to drink, dance and listen to music. Picturing all these people streaming into her restaurant brought a smile to her face as she made her way toward the bar. Before she reached it, however, someone asked, "Is that smile for me?" before spinning her onto the dance floor.

Chapter Four

For one horrifying moment, Lauren thought it was Phil who'd grabbed her. Even when she looked up into the face of Tim Wainwright, it still took several moments for her heart to start its descent back to its proper place in her chest from her throat.

"Glad to see you came out to enjoy the nightlife," Tim said.

"Can't say I expected to be accosted as a result."

Tim's eyebrows lifted. "Accosted? I merely meant to claim the first dance before a line formed."

She rolled her eyes. "No need to butter me up. I'm not closer to making a decision about vendors than I was a few days ago."

"Did I say anything about beef?"

She hesitated a moment as he spun her expertly between two couples to avoid a collision that could result in a pile of cowboy hats and boots. Even Tim was dressed in jeans, boots and Stetson tonight. If she wasn't a born-and-bred Texan, she might actually buy that he was a real cowboy.

"No," she finally said.

"I'm off the clock and just wanted to dance with a pretty woman."

She doubted he was ever really off the clock, but what could one dance hurt? It wasn't as if it was a date, or would lead to one.

"Just a bit of friendly advice—perhaps ask for the dance next time rather than assume." Sure, she wanted to make friends here, but his action had rubbed her the wrong way.

He nodded. "Duly noted. I'm sorry."

She simply offered a polite smile in return, not the "It's okay" he possibly expected. Once upon a time she might have uttered it without thinking, but that was before the events of the past year and a half.

"So, how are you liking Blue Falls so far?" he asked.

Thankful to have a neutral topic to discuss, she said, "I really like it. The people are nice, and it has a great feel to the business district. Not to mention it's pretty."

"Glad to hear it."

Lauren began to relax and even allowed Tim to lead her around the dance floor for a second song. Occasionally, she spotted someone she'd met over the course of the past few days. Thank goodness Verona Charles didn't seem to be in attendance. She didn't need the woman getting any ideas about her and Tim. If Tim or Verona headed down that path, Lauren was going to break out her stockpile of stories about poopy diapers and buying teething gel in bulk.

Her breath caught unexpectedly when she spotted Adam Hartley sitting at the bar. Tim spun her around so quickly that she wasn't sure, but she thought Adam had been watching them. And while her gaze had met his only for the briefest of moments, it was long enough for her to get the impression he wasn't pleased.

Most likely it was because he'd seen her dancing

with his competitor and feared he'd lost the contract with her. Was he just another guy who'd been nice to her for his own gain? For some reason, the idea of that trait applying to Adam bothered her more than if that was what Tim was doing. Maybe it was because she expected it from Tim from the moment she met him. But she should know better than anybody that it was the ones you didn't expect that posed the biggest threat.

Still, she really hadn't gotten that vibe from Adam, even though she'd been looking for it. That she might have been gravely mistaken again caused her mood to dampen, enough that after the song was finished she excused herself from the dance floor.

"Maybe we can do this again sometime," Tim said as she stepped away.

"It's a small town, so I'm sure we'll see each other here at some point." She saw her noncommittal answer register with him a moment before she turned away and headed for the bar.

She told herself it was to purchase a drink, not to orchestrate a meeting with Adam. But she wasn't very good at lying to herself. The truth was she liked him, and had she not been so recently burned she might be interested in him for reasons beyond friendship. He certainly was attractive, and he'd gotten a seal of approval from the Bryants. But at this stage in her life, she needed to focus on her family, her business and healing herself. Her soul still felt bruised and battered by Phil's betrayal. And she couldn't even think about being with anyone else until that wasn't the case anymore.

Truthfully, with her daughters to consider now, she didn't know if it was possible to trust anyone enough to risk not only her own heart, but also those of her precious babies. They were too young now to realize their father wanted nothing to do with them, so Lauren tried her best to shower them with the love of two parents.

By the time she reached the bar area, she no longer saw Adam. She glanced around but couldn't find him in the crowd, which seemed to have gotten bigger during the time she'd been on the dance floor. Had he left? Maybe that was for the best. No, it was *definitely* for the best. She attributed the unexpected pull toward him as a side effect of being in a new place where she didn't really know anyone, being away from the familiarity and comfort of home, and the frustrating human desire to feel wanted for the right reasons.

A moment after she claimed one of the bar stools, the bartender stepped up in front of her. "What can I get for you?"

She glanced at the menu board above the shelves of liquor bottles. "Just a lemonade."

"Coming right up."

"So, I hear you're going to be my new competition."

Lauren turned to see a pretty woman not more than a few years older than her and quickly deduced her identity.

"Keri Teague, right?"

The sense of apprehension tightening Lauren's muscles eased the moment Keri smiled. "In the flesh."

"I hear you are known far and wide as quite the baker."

"Not as far as you, but I do all right."

"Well, as I told someone earlier this week, I don't think there can ever be too many baked goods within close proximity."

Keri laughed. "We're going to get along just fine."

"You don't know how glad I am to hear that."

"Don't tell me that you thought I'd be an ogre. Okay, who's been telling stories about me?"

"Nothing bad," Lauren said. "Adam Hartley just said I might have some friendly competition."

"That's a fair assessment. Good, I won't have to have him arrested."

Lauren felt her eyebrows shoot upward. "Arrested?"

Keri laughed. "Sorry, guess no one told you I'm married to the sheriff and that I get a kick out of teasing people about having him arrest them."

"Uh, no. But I'll be sure to be on my best behavior."

The bartender delivered Lauren's lemonade in a big frosty glass.

"So how do you know Adam?" Keri asked.

"He came by to pitch his family's beef products."

"You going with them?"

"Haven't decided yet. That's a ways down the road."

Keri nodded as if she totally understood, which she probably did since she also ran a food-related business and likely got unsolicited visits from vendors all the time, as well.

"Adam's good people."

"So I keep hearing."

Keri gave her a questioning look, but Lauren pretended not to notice. She didn't know how many of the locals Verona Charles had in league with her on the whole matchmaking thing.

"I saw him a little while ago. Not sure where he got off to." Keri scanned the crowd, and again Lauren pretended not to notice. "Oh, he's out on the dance floor."

He was? Though she was curious as to the identity of his dance partner, Lauren had the presence of mind not to look. Instead, she steered the conversation with Keri in a different direction, asking how long she'd owned the bakery.

For the next few minutes, they shared stories about everything from baking disasters and successes to the inside scoop on various locals. To be honest, with a single conversation and a lot of laughs, Lauren felt more a part of the community. But when she glanced at her phone, she was surprised by how much time had passed.

"I better get going," she said.

"So soon. You barely made use of the dance floor."

"Been a long day. Going to be another one tomorrow."

Keri nodded in understanding. "Well, come by the bakery sometime soon and I'll give you a little treat on the house."

As she thanked Keri and stood to leave, she deliberately didn't check the dance floor or any of the surrounding tables for Adam. One would think after what she'd gone through with Phil, the part of her brain wired to notice attractive men would have been out of order. Evidently not. Thank goodness she had enough sense not to indulge it too far.

As she made her way through the crowd, she felt as if someone was watching her. Though she said she wouldn't, she directed her attention toward the dance floor. Adam was still out there, but he wasn't looking her way. She scanned the sea of faces and didn't see anything out of the ordinary. She shook her head, telling herself not to be so paranoid, and resumed her trek toward the exit.

The moment she stepped outside and the door closed behind her, it was as if someone had turned down a blaring radio to its lowest volume. She could still hear the music inside, but her ears thanked her for the comparative silence of the surrounding night.

It'd gotten chillier since she went inside, so she zipped up her jacket and quickly texted her mom that she was on her way back. She headed across the parking lot, glancing up at the blanket of stars above.

"Well, ain't you a pretty one?"

Her heart leaped immediately to her throat at the sound of the man's voice. Her brain supplied the extra bit of information that he'd had too much to drink and that he wasn't alone. From the look on the other man's face, he was equally inebriated. Neither of them was a small man. Rather, they looked as if they could wrestle a full-size bull to the ground.

Blue Falls seemed so friendly and safe that she hadn't once thought being out after dark by herself would be dangerous, but she supposed there were drunk jerks everywhere. Which was little consolation at the moment. With most of the downtown businesses closed and the noise level inside the music hall, she doubted anyone would even hear her scream.

Her babies' faces flashed through her mind. Thank goodness they were safe with her mother.

"What, you can't speak?" the second guy asked, taking a couple of steps toward her, prompting her to take three backward and hoping she didn't trip over her own feet.

At first she hesitated to take her eyes off the men. But she knew she couldn't get past them, so her only choice was to get back to the safety of the throng of people inside the building. She shot a quick glance toward the entrance, judging how quickly she could make it. *If* she could make it.

As if her thundering heart had willed it, the door to the hall opened…and out stepped none other than Adam Hartley.

ADAM HAD DANCED to a few songs with Courtney Heard, a friend from high school, and her cousin, Shannon, who was visiting from El Paso, but as he left the music hall he found his mood hadn't improved to any great extent. He wasn't sure if the sour feeling in his middle was because Lauren had been dancing with someone else, or the fact that the someone else was Tim Wainwright. He'd found himself wondering if Lauren was really averse to dating someone new, or if smooth-talking Tim had already managed to change her mind.

He should have stayed home tonight, but the realization that he was the only adult member of the family who didn't have someone—significant other, child or both—had him itching to get out and do something. Blue Falls nightlife being what it was, he'd had two choices—the Frothy Stein bar or the music hall. Deciding the Stein was the more pathetic of the two, he'd headed for the music hall to see who was playing tonight. The band from Austin was pretty good, and the crowd had helped him shake off the "odd man out" feeling. At least until he'd seen Lauren in Tim's arms on the dance floor. When she'd smiled up at Tim, Adam felt as if a bit too much of his siblings' newfound affinity for happily ever after had rubbed off on him.

When finding his own dance partners hadn't helped, he'd said his good-nights and headed for the exit. But who did he see as soon as he stepped out into the crisp night air? One Lauren Shayne. His momentary "you've got to be kidding me" was immediately replaced by the realization that she was wild-eyed scared. The two hefty guys encroaching on her personal space was obviously the reason why.

Wasting no time, he ate up the distance between them. He'd take on both guys if he had to in order to protect her, even knowing he'd likely be the worse for it after everything was over.

"There you are," he said, swooping in next to Lauren and wrapping his arm around her waist. "Sorry. I got caught up inside."

She stiffened next to him, but must have realized what he was doing because she relaxed slightly the next moment.

"Get your own," one of the guys said, his breath evidence he'd fail a field sobriety test.

"Already did, and you're making her uncomfortable. Why don't you all go inside and ask the bartender for some coffee?" And give Adam time to get Lauren safely away from their meaty claws, not to mention make a call to the sheriff's office to keep these two off the roads tonight.

The two drunks glanced at each other, and it was as if Adam could read their minds.

"Don't even think about it."

Adam didn't know if his warning swayed them or the fact that the door to the music hall opened, spilling out light as well as half a dozen patrons. Whatever the reason, they backed off but cursed as they headed toward the other end of the parking lot. But Adam didn't relinquish his hold on Lauren as he asked her where she was parked.

"I walked here from the Wildflower Inn."

"Then I guess it's my turn to give you a lift."

"Thanks. I'd appreciate that."

He noticed Lauren glance back over her shoulder as he escorted her toward his truck, as if she was afraid the guys would change their minds again and attack them from behind. Once they reached his truck, he opened the passenger door for her.

"Sorry to inconvenience you," she said once she was in the seat and pulling her seat belt across her body.

"It's not a problem. I drive right past the inn on the way home."

"Oh, good."

He hurried around to the driver's side and hit the door locks as soon as he shut his door, giving Lauren an extra layer of protection from her would-be attackers.

"If you don't mind, I'm going to call the sheriff's office first. Those two," he said, pointing toward the men, who now appeared to be arguing, "don't need to be on the road endangering people."

"Good idea."

A sheriff's department vehicle pulled up to the edge of the parking lot before he even got off the phone. Sheriff Simon Teague got out of his cruiser at the same time a department SUV also arrived.

"Is one of those the sheriff?" Lauren asked.

"Yeah, the one already out of his car."

"I met his wife tonight."

"Should we expect the bake-off at the O.K. Corral?"

As he'd hoped, she laughed. "No, Keri's very nice. And despite your teasing me about her competition, she had only nice things to say about you. So do the Bryants. Seems you're 'good people.'"

"Had I given the impression that I wasn't?"

"No. They were completely unsolicited comments."

"It's always good to hear people think well of you, I guess."

He started his truck's engine and left the music hall and the law enforcement activity behind.

"How did you like your first trip to the music hall? I assume it's your first visit anyway."

"It was. Had no intention of going, but I was out for a walk and got drawn in by the music. Nice place, but I think I was just too tired to be in the mood to dance the night away."

She'd seemed to be having a good time with Tim, but he reminded himself that she had practice putting on a friendly face. He'd seen it with the women in the café. At least she hadn't left with Tim. Although her leaving alone had nearly cost her dearly. He squeezed the steering wheel harder, almost wishing the guys had thrown a punch or two at him so he could give it right back. A cold chill went through him just thinking about what might have happened if he hadn't decided to head home when he had.

"I hope you don't let those guys sour your opinion of Blue Falls."

"No. Unfortunately, it doesn't matter how big or small a place is, there are going to be drunken brutes at some point or another."

She was making a valiant effort to not seem too concerned about what had just happened, but he noticed how she had her hands clasped tightly together in her lap. Before he could think better of it, he reached across and gave her arm a reassuring squeeze.

"You're safe now."

He removed his hand after only a moment, not wanting her to fear she'd traded one scary situation for another, and turned in to the inn's lot. He pulled up to the front entrance so she'd only have to walk a few steps to get inside.

"Thank you for the ride. And for helping me out with those guys. I was afraid they were going to jump you."

He grinned. "I'd have made them wish they hadn't."

"You might have gotten in some good licks, but there were two of them and they seemed like the type who'd tackle a *chupacabra* wearing a cactus coat just for the hell of it."

He laughed at that colorful description. "Can't say I've heard that one before."

"It's a Lauren Shayne original. Just now thought of it."

"Somebody ought to draw that and put it on T-shirts. They'd probably sell like beer on the Fourth of July."

"Seriously, though, thank you."

"You're welcome. I doubt you have any more trouble from them, but if you do let me know. We've got enough Hartleys to form a posse."

"I appreciate the offer, but I don't think we have to go full-on Old West." She had her door open in the next breath, then stepped out. "Good night, Adam."

"Good night, Lauren."

He didn't move until he was sure she was safely inside. It wasn't until he was halfway home that he realized he'd been replaying how his name sounded when she said it. And that he'd been imagining her standing much closer to him, looking up into his eyes with the type of interest that had nothing to do with business contracts.

Yep, he was up crazy creek without a paddle.

Chapter Five

As Lauren stepped into the lobby of the inn, she was startled to come face-to-face with Papa Ed. He nodded toward the door, and quite possibly where Adam still was to make sure she got inside safely.

"Who was that?"

"One of the vendors I met earlier in the week. I took a walk through the downtown area, and he gave me a lift back up here."

"That was nice of him." There was no mistaking the tone of her grandfather's voice. It was much more a question than a statement of fact. But she wasn't about to tell him what had happened to precipitate the front-door drop-off.

"Yeah. You were right. People are nice here." With the exception of the two guys who were now hopefully either spending the night in the drunk tank, or were at least in need of a ride of their own because the sheriff had taken their keys away.

Papa Ed gave her one of his looks that said he knew there was more to the story and if he just watched her long enough she'd reveal all. She pretended she didn't notice and instead nodded at the package of little chocolate doughnuts in his hand.

"Munchies?"

He lifted the package and looked at it, then lowered it again as if disappointed in himself. "I know it's not fine eating, but they're a guilty pleasure."

"Plus you already ate all the snacks I brought along."

"It's your fault. If they weren't so good, there'd be plenty left."

She smiled and laughed a little. "And I wouldn't have the career I do."

"True. But at least those little girls give me plenty of ways to stay active and keep the weight at bay."

"Speaking of, I better go relieve Mom. I was gone longer than I anticipated."

"Any particular reason why?"

She'd opened herself back up to the questioning she'd managed to divert him from, dang it. Might as well tell the truth—at least the nonscary part of it.

"I wanted to walk along Main Street when there weren't a lot of people around, and I ended up stopping by the music hall. Thought it was a good idea to start meeting other local business owners. I did meet the owner of the local bakery, Keri Teague, and we talked longer than I planned to be gone."

No need to mention the dancing with Tim or how she'd headed to the bar in order to say hello to Adam, or how the night could have come to a very different end were it not for his fortuitous timing. She barely controlled a shiver down her spine at that train of thought.

"So, your chauffeur back—he the one you said was a little too full of himself, or the one who helped you move the furniture?"

Evidently Violet had spilled the details Lauren had shared with her during one of their phone calls.

"Furniture."

"Hmm, he *is* a nice guy."

Thankfully, Lauren yawned then, and she hadn't even resorted to faking it. Her long day was catching up with her.

"I need to hit the hay. I have an early meeting with an electrician in the morning."

Papa Ed and his processed snack accompanied her down the hall. She gave him a quick peck on the cheek before opening the door to her room. By the quiet that greeted her, she knew the girls were already asleep. Her mom was sitting in bed wearing her pajamas and reading the latest mystery in a series she liked about a baker who solved crimes. Lauren always found it odd that a baker happened upon so many dead bodies.

Lauren eased her way over to the crib and her heart filled at the sight that greeted her. Harper and Bethany were sound asleep with their little hands touching. She couldn't imagine it being possible to love another human more than she loved her babies. She longed to kiss them both, but she didn't want to risk waking them—especially in a hotel room where the other occupants might not be thrilled with the sound of crying infants.

When she turned away from the temptation of snuggling the girls, she said, "Sorry I was gone so long."

"It's no problem, hon. See anything interesting?"

Adam Hartley.

In another life, maybe.

"Some nice shops downtown I'll explore when I have some time." She almost laughed at the idea of having free time before giving her mom the same version of events at the music hall that she'd given Papa Ed.

"Sounds as if Dad might be trying to edge you back into the dating game."

Surprised by her mom's assessment, Lauren looked over at her. "Why would he do that? He knows men aren't high on my favorites list right now."

"He believes people shouldn't go through life alone. He did the same thing to me a couple of years after your father died. It took Dad a long time to realize I wasn't interested in dating again. I had my girls, my teaching career, a life that was satisfying if, admittedly, sometimes a little lonely."

Lauren's heart squeezed. Her mom hadn't ever admitted to that loneliness before.

"But what happened to me wasn't the same thing. Dad didn't choose to leave you." It had been an accident on an icy road, not anyone's fault unless you chose to blame Mother Nature or God.

"I think Dad felt guilty, or maybe just sad, that what your father and I had was cut short while he and Mom were happy all through their long marriage. He was happy and so he wanted everyone around him to be happy, too."

The pain Papa Ed must be going through without Nana Gloria hit Lauren anew. Still, she couldn't imagine her grandfather thinking she'd be the least bit interested in a new relationship, even a casual one. When would she even have time for such a thing?

And yet there was that little flicker of attraction that had led her to the bar in search of Adam Hartley. How did she explain that? Maybe it was possible to still feel physical attraction without wanting anything to come from it. If she was being honest, she didn't know how a woman couldn't be at least somewhat attracted to

Adam. Based on her few interactions with him, he was a very pleasing blend of handsome, kind, helpful and dedicated to family and honest work. That was a difficult cocktail to not want to drink in one delicious gulp. Not that she had much opportunity for cocktails these days, either.

"Considering everything, I'm happier than people might expect. Who could complain when they have an awesome job, a great family and two beautiful, healthy baby girls?" And if she sometimes felt lonely while lying alone in her bed, it was a small price to pay for all the other positive things in her life.

"I might seem a hypocrite for saying this, but don't rule out having more when you're ready. Contrary to what Dad may think, I didn't. I just never met anyone else I could imagine spending my life with. I suppose I still could, but I stopped thinking that way quite some time ago. But you're still young."

"With two babies. Most guys aren't into instant family."

"Maybe not, but someone might surprise you."

That would be a surprise indeed. But then she thought about the look on Adam's face when he talked about his family, about his nieces and nephews. Maybe guys who didn't mind being around other people's kids did exist, but it would have to be a special man indeed to make her willing to take a chance again. He might have to be miraculous.

INSTEAD OF TURNING right out of the inn's parking lot, Adam drove back down into the main part of town. There was no sign of either of the guys who'd frightened Lauren in front of the music hall anymore—or law enforcement for that matter. So he headed toward the sheriff's office, intent on making sure those two didn't pose a threat to Lauren or anyone else. Though he'd wanted to teach them a lesson they wouldn't forget, he'd had enough sense to know he was outnumbered. If only his brothers had been with him. He wasn't by nature a violent person, but he'd seen bright red when he'd realized what was happening when he stepped outside the music hall. Thank God he'd left when he had. It didn't escape him that Lauren—or rather his reaction to seeing her with Tim—was what had made him decide to vacate the premises.

As he cruised up to the sheriff's office, he spotted Simon coming out of the building. When he pulled in next to the sheriff, he rolled down his window.

"Please tell me those idiots are sleeping it off in a cell tonight."

Simon crossed his arms. "I'll do you one better. They managed to get themselves arrested. The bigger fella decided it might be fun to take a swing at me. I disavowed him of that notion."

Adam smiled wide. "You just made my night."

"Any reason you're extra interested in them?"

"When I came out of the building, they were about to attack Lauren Shayne."

The look on Simon's face hardened. "I should talk to her."

Adam instinctually shook his head. "They never touched her, just scared the living daylights out of her. But it looked like it was about to go further when I intervened. Honestly, I was probably about to get my ass kicked, but some other people came out before anything happened."

"So I get the impression Miss Shayne doesn't want to be involved any further in this?"

"No." She hadn't actually said that out loud, but he'd somehow managed to read that in her body language. She'd only wanted to leave. "I just wanted to make sure they wouldn't be a problem anymore, for anyone."

It wasn't only about Lauren. His sisters sometimes had a night out at the music hall. Also female friends, tourists and barrel racers in town for the regular rodeos.

"I suspect when they sober up, they'll make bail and go back to Johnsonville and choose to party elsewhere next time around."

"Good."

"So, you already making a move on the pretty baker lady? Got to say from experience that being with a woman that good with desserts is not a bad bonus."

"No, I just happened to be in the right place at the right time to help her out."

"Her knight in shining armor, huh?"

Adam rolled his eyes. "Good night, Simon," he said, then drove away.

As he passed by the inn, he glanced over as if he might catch a glimpse of Lauren. But he doubted after her experience with the drunks that she'd step foot back outside until the sun was well above the horizon.

And when that time came, he needed to be hard at work doing anything but thinking about how he'd been wishing she was dancing with him instead of his biggest rival.

LAUREN DIDN'T THINK she'd ever been so happy to see a sunrise, despite the fact her night had been filled with some of the worst, most interrupted sleep ever. If she wasn't having nightmares about what could have happened outside the music hall if Adam hadn't shown up when he had, she was being awakened—likely along with everyone else in the hotel—by not one but both of the girls crying. It seemed her precious girls were similar in more ways than one, including when they were upset by hunger, wet diapers or the pains of teething. The challenge was trying to get them to stop crying at the same time. Neither seemed to want to be first in that regard. At home it was one thing, but knowing their upset was bothering other people trying to get a good night's sleep frayed Lauren's nerves. Keeping a hotel full of people awake wasn't the best way to win friends and future customers.

When her mom came out of the bathroom, she looked as worn out as Lauren felt.

"Pardon me for saying this," Lauren said, keeping quiet since the girls were actually sleeping peacefully now, "but it doesn't look as if the shower helped much."

Her mom rubbed her hand over her face. "It's been a few years since I've had babies crying their lungs out, and I only had one at a time. You, my dear, are a saint."

She didn't feel like a saint. More like exhausted before the day even started.

"I hate to leave you here with them again today."

Her mom waved off her concern. "I'll let them sleep now, then we'll come down to visit later. Dad and I can lend a hand if you'll let us."

"Normally, I'd say I'm good, but today I may take you up on it." Though it might be nice just to have the quiet and solitude for a few hours. She loved her girls more than life itself, but she'd bet every cent she had that there wasn't a mother alive who didn't want to run away from her children for a little bit every now and then.

Though when she arrived at the restaurant building a few minutes later, she didn't immediately get out of her car. Instead, she fought an uncharacteristic wave of anxiety. What if those guys were inside waiting on her to finish what they'd started? She thought about Adam's business card in her wallet and considered texting him to see if he knew what had happened to the men after they left. But why would he? He'd been going home after he dropped her off, and it wasn't as if the drunks had actually attacked either of them. Thus, no need to have further contact with the sheriff's department.

Taking a deep breath, she told herself that the faster she got in that building and to work, the sooner she and her family could go home. And the thought of letting any other man halt her forward progress sent enough anger through her that it propelled her out of the car and into the blessedly empty building.

She did lock the door behind her this time, but keeping out anyone who could just wander in made sense. Despite her lack of sleep, she managed to get some of the windows cleaned before the electrician arrived. By the time he finished his inspection, however, she was back to wondering what she'd gotten herself into. It was going to take more work to bring things up to code than she'd hoped. The news knocked what little energy she'd mustered right out of her. After the electrician left, she sank onto an old metal bench outside the front door and dropped her head into her hands.

She didn't look up until she heard footsteps approaching. The shot of fear was quickly replaced when she noticed her visitor was Adam. Again, he'd arrived on foot.

"Don't tell me you hit another deer," she said.

"No." He motioned diagonally across the street to the Shop Mart. "Coming back from Austin. I had to stop and get a couple of things for my dad."

She recognized his truck at the edge of the other lot.

"Are you okay?" he asked as he sank onto the identical bench on the opposite side of the front walkway from her. "Excuse me for saying so, but you look as if you didn't sleep last night."

"That's because I didn't, not much anyway."

"Maybe you should take a day off."

She shook her head. "Don't have the time."

"Then how about some help? What do you need?"

"Adam, you've already helped me more than anybody in town." She hadn't consciously realized just how much until she said it out loud. "I'm sure you have your own work to do."

"Not so much that I can't spare a few hours."

"I wouldn't feel right—"

He held up a hand. "You're not going to win this argument, so you might as well put me to work."

She lifted an eyebrow. "And here everyone has been telling me you're a nice guy, but you've got a bossy streak."

He smiled, and she tried to pretend she hadn't felt a flutter in her middle.

Lauren gave up. And if she admitted the truth, she liked having him around. Though he caused her to have unexpected reactions, he was also easy to be around. With each interaction, she was beginning to believe more and more that everyone who said he was a genuinely nice guy was telling the truth. He'd given her no reason to believe otherwise. As long as she didn't allow herself to admire him too much, she'd be okay.

"So, do you do windows?" she asked.

Lauren couldn't believe how much quicker her work progressed with just one extra set of hands. And though she'd still had the same pitiful amount of sleep, having Adam there to talk to made her feel more awake. Granted, that could be the bit of adrenaline still zinging its way through her body after they'd nearly bumped into each other and he'd instinctively placed his hand on her bare arm to steady her. It had been nothing more than a brief touch, and yet she'd swear in a court of law she could still feel his strong, warm fingers against her flesh.

She glanced up to where he stood on the ladder, washing the windows up high. Well, he was supposed to be washing them. It appeared that he was instead writing in the accumulated dust with his finger.

"What are you doing?"

Instead of answering, he shot her a mischievous grin. She pictured a little-boy version of him smiling that same way after some naughty misadventure.

Lauren took a few steps back in order to read what he'd written. *I should get free meals for life for doing this. Including dessert.*

"I don't know. That would depend on how long you're planning on living. What's the longevity like in your family?"

His smile dimmed, and she felt like kicking herself. Life and death wasn't something to joke about, especially when there was the possibility of loss associated with the subject. She ought to know that from experience.

"I'm sorry." She wasn't even sure how to articulate the rest of what she was thinking.

"It's okay. I'm adopted so my parents' genetics don't have any bearing on mine."

"Oh." But what about his birth parents? His grandparents? If he was adopted, did that mean they weren't around anymore? And hadn't been since he was a kid?

Adam proceeded to wash away the humorous words from the window, and it made her inexplicably sad. It was as if the moment a bit of humor strolled into her life, she found a way to erase it.

When he was finished washing the high-up windows, Adam descended the ladder and came over to the front counter, where she was standing sketching out ideas for the placement of customer seating and the gift-shop area. The thoughts that had been eating at her the past few minutes found their way out of her mouth.

"I really am sorry if I brought up bad memories. I should have thought before I spoke."

"It's really okay. It happened a long time ago."

She started to ask what but managed to stop herself. It wasn't any of her business.

"You don't have to be so careful around me," he said. "I won't break."

She looked up at him and realized again just how much she liked him already. If she hadn't been through what she had with Phil, she wouldn't even question her assessment of Adam. She hated that she now always looked for hidden meaning behind words, selfish intent behind actions.

"My birth parents died in a bridge collapse when I

was six. I went to live with my grandmother after that for a year, but then she had a stroke and had to be moved to a care facility."

Without any conscious thought, she placed her hand atop his on the counter. "I'm so sorry." That was a lot of loss to deal with. "I lost my dad when I was five, but I can't imagine losing both parents at once."

"I won't lie and say it wasn't hard, but I got lucky in the end. My parents now are great, and I ended up with brothers and sisters instead of being an only child. They're all adopted, too, so I wasn't alone in that experience, either."

"How many of you are there?"

"Five. Neil, Ben and Sloane are older, and Angel is younger."

"That's amazing that your parents adopted so many kids."

"We tease them that they like to collect strays."

Lauren smiled at that and wondered what life was like when all the Hartleys got together. Just then the door opened, revealing Papa Ed and her mother pushing the double stroller. Lauren realized her hand was still lying atop the masculine warmth of Adam's and she pulled it away, so quickly that it made her appear as if she'd been doing something wrong.

"Hey," she said to the new arrivals, probably sounding way brighter and cheerier than she should.

She didn't miss the curious glances both her mother and Papa Ed leveled at Adam. Before their imaginations ran wild, she gestured toward Adam.

"You're just in time to see what a great job Adam did on washing the windows."

"You hired someone?" her mother asked.

Lauren shook her head. "No, Adam was kind enough to help with the stuff up high."

"This the young man who drove you back last night?" Papa Ed asked.

"Yes. Adam Hartley, this is my grandfather, Ed, and my mom, Jeanie." And now for the part of the introductions that would likely have her seeing the backside of Adam as he suddenly had to be somewhere else. She reminded herself that was okay. "And these two sleeping beauties are my daughters, Harper and Bethany."

Instead of causing a blur as he ran for the exit, Adam crossed the few feet that separated him from the stroller. Lauren held her breath for some reason. When he smiled as he crouched down in front of them, she inexplicably felt like crying happy tears.

"They sure do look as if they don't have a care in the world, don't they?"

Lauren couldn't help the sudden laugh. "Don't let their cherubic faces fool you. They both have an incredible lung capacity, which they put to good use last night."

Adam looked up at her. "That explains why you're so tired."

"You don't know the half of it." There was so much, so very much, behind that simple statement. And to her great surprise, Adam didn't run away. In fact, if she didn't know better she'd swear he'd be perfectly willing to listen to every gory detail. And a bigger surprise than anything was that down deep, a part of her wanted to tell him.

Not trusting herself or the part of her brain that had evidently forgotten the past eighteen months, she shifted her attention to her mom. "Let me show you around."

She forced herself not to look back at Adam again as

she led her mom toward the area of the building where the gift shop would eventually be located.

"It certainly has a lovely view," her mom said as she looked out the now-clean windows a couple of minutes later.

"Yeah, that was a big selling point."

Her mom glanced back toward the front of the building, where Lauren could hear Adam talking to Papa Ed but couldn't tell what they were saying. She realized she hadn't warned Adam not to say anything about the two guys outside the music hall. Hopefully, he wouldn't divulge that bit of information she purposely hadn't shared with her family.

"Can't say the view of the other direction is bad, either."

"Mom!" Lauren miraculously kept her voice low enough that she didn't attract the attention of the men.

"What? Am I lying?"

Well, no. Not by a long shot. "He's just being friendly, nothing more."

Her mom gave her one of those "mom" looks that said she was highly suspicious there was something Lauren wasn't telling her.

"Did I say otherwise?"

Damn it. Lauren realized she'd just revealed more than she wanted to admit to herself. She was really attracted to Adam, and not just because he was pleasing to the eye. The part of her that still ached from Phil's betrayal was looking for a balm, and it seemed to want that balm to be named Adam Hartley.

"You don't have to completely turn off your feelings, hon," her mom said. "Use caution, yes, but don't allow yourself to live the rest of your life afraid."

"I barely know him."

"I'm not saying he's the one or if there even is a 'one,' just that I don't want you to let Phil burrow too deeply into your mind. He's not worth it."

She was right about that, but that didn't mean she had any idea how to not let the experience with him color how she responded to people going forward.

Not wanting Adam to realize they were talking about him and perhaps get the wrong idea, she walked back across the building. As they drew close, Harper woke up and her gaze fixed on the tall, handsome man in front of her.

"Well, hello there, cutie," Adam said.

Lauren smiled at the genuine tenderness in his voice. At least it sounded genuine. Surely he wouldn't use fake affection for her children as another way to influence her to do business with him.

Harper smiled and wiggled her feet at the same time she thrust out her arms toward him. Lauren couldn't have been more surprised if her daughter had unhooked herself from the stroller and proceeded to walk across to the windows for a view of the lake.

"Well, will you look at that?" Papa Ed said.

Adam looked confused.

"She's never done anything like that with someone who isn't family," Lauren said. "Neither of them has."

"Do you mind if I hold her? I'll be careful."

"Uh, sure."

Lauren reached down to release the lap belt, but Adam already had it freed and was lifting Harper into his arms. Lauren resisted the urge to stand close in case he dropped his happy bundle. He must have seen the worry on her face because he smiled.

"Don't worry. I have lots of practice. I'm an uncle, remember?"

She had to admit he looked as if he knew what he was doing. He tapped the pad of his finger against the tip of Harper's nose and said, "Boop." Evidently, Harper found that hilarious because she let out a belly laugh before planting her little palm against Adam's nose.

Lauren was pretty sure her ovaries struck up a lively tune and started tap dancing. Not good. Not good at all.

"I think she likes you," Papa Ed said.

As if she didn't like being left out, Bethany woke up and started fussing. Knowing her ovaries couldn't handle seeing both of her babies in Adam's arms, Lauren picked up Bethany and proceeded to do a little dance with her. It had the desired effect of replacing the eminent tears with a precious baby grin.

Adam reached over and booped Bethany's nose the same as he had Harper's and got a similar result.

"Okay, stop trying to become their favorite human," Lauren said. "That's my title."

"Can't help it. They must smell the spoiling uncle on me."

Lauren had the craziest thought that she didn't want him to be their uncle. But she couldn't allow herself to even think he'd be anything more than just a funny guy who made them laugh. There were so many reasons to demand her ovaries knock off the dancing.

But, seriously, how was she supposed to ignore how sexy the man looked holding her daughter and making the babies laugh? That was impossible. Even women who didn't want children would darn near melt at the sight. Women with eyes and any shred of maternal instinct didn't stand a chance.

ADAM WASN'T QUITE sure how to interpret the look on Lauren's face. It was almost as if she couldn't believe what she was seeing. Did she think he'd hurt her babies somehow? Was she surprised he actually liked kids? He guessed he should have expected that kind of reaction. After all, he'd witnessed how protective his sisters and sisters-in-law were of their children. And he knew enough guys who didn't want anything to do with kids, especially if they weren't their own.

It hit him that the twins' father must be the ex-fiancé who'd dragged Lauren into court. Did she have to continue to deal with him for their daughters' sake? He couldn't imagine being forced to speak to someone he couldn't stand for the next couple of decades.

"How many nieces and nephews do you have?" Lauren's mother asked.

"Two nieces and one nephew for now, but there's another on the way."

"Big family?"

"Yeah. One big, cobbled-together family."

At Jeanie's look of confusion, Lauren explained, "Adam and his four siblings are all adopted."

"From different families," he added, realizing he hadn't revealed that detail before.

"Well, bless your parents," Jeanie said.

He smiled. "I'm sure there were times when they wondered what they'd gotten themselves into."

"I think all parents wonder that from time to time."

Lauren made an expression of mock affront. "I don't know what you're talking about, Mom. Granted, Violet was a pill, but I was perfect."

Her mom actually snorted at that. "Just like you

thought these two were without fault about four this morning."

Adam jostled Harper, causing her to grin and reveal the hint of a tiny tooth about to make its appearance.

"I don't know what these people are talking about," he said to the little girl. "You seem pretty perfect to me."

This time, all three of the other adults were looking at him as if he was a unicorn.

Almost as if they all realized what they were doing at the same time, their expressions changed as they redirected their attention.

"Well, I should probably be heading out," Adam said as he handed over Harper to her grandmother.

"Don't run on our account," Jeanie said. "At least let us treat you to lunch."

"No need, but thank you." Even though he needed to get back to the ranch, he found himself not wanting to leave. Maybe that was why he found himself extending an invitation. "Why don't you all come out to the ranch for dinner while you're here?"

"We wouldn't want to intrude," Lauren replied quickly.

Had he overstepped somehow? Or was she just being polite? One way to find out.

"No imposition. My mom loves having people over. Like I said, she loves your show, so I might even win some 'favorite son' points if I bring you all over for dinner."

Lauren hesitated. It was her grandfather who answered for all of them.

"Well, in that case, we'd be happy to accept." Both Lauren and her mother looked at Ed with surprise, but Lauren was quick to refocus her attention on Adam.

"Thank you. We appreciate it. Hopefully you'll have the same calming effect on Harper and Bethany then." Even though she was nice, he got the feeling she was worried. If she thought a couple of crying babies would bother his family, she was mistaken.

"If I don't, someone will be able to."

As he finally headed for the door a couple of minutes later, he still had the feeling Lauren was on edge. He was honestly surprised she accompanied him outside.

"Thanks again for your help today," she said.

"It was nothing." Despite not being a great fan of washing windows, he'd enjoyed spending time with her. "Listen, I'm sorry if inviting you and your family to dinner made you uncomfortable."

She shook her head. "No, it's okay. That's just a lot of people to invite without asking your mother first."

He laughed. "I could bring home an entire tour bus full of flower peepers and she'd be in hog heaven. We've joked that when we all eventually move out, she's probably going to turn the house into a bed-and-breakfast."

"At least let me bring something. I can bake a cake."

"Where?" He pointed toward the building. "You don't have an operational kitchen yet. Plus, Mom isn't a slouch when it comes to dessert, so no worries there."

Finally, Lauren looked marginally more comfortable with the idea of eating with a family of strangers.

"I promise we don't bite," he said.

She smiled at that, and he found himself wanting to do more to make her smile. "I can't say the same for the girls. Teething makes them want to chew on whatever is handy."

"Then we'll make sure the dog's chew toys aren't within their reach."

He became aware of her mother and grandfather inside, watching them while trying to seem as if they weren't. "Well, see you tomorrow night."

"Okay. And—"

"Don't you dare thank me again."

She made a show of pressing her lips together but he could still see the gratitude in her eyes. Though he didn't need her thanks, it was nicer to see than suspicion.

As he walked across the street to his truck, he tried not to think about other emotions he wouldn't mind seeing in Lauren's eyes.

Chapter Six

Adam walked into the dining room where his mom was busy wrapping Christmas presents. Rolls of colorful paper, tape, tags and scissors were scattered across the surface of the table.

"Any of that for me?"

"No, this is all for the kids. I have to sneak my wrapping in when they aren't here."

He wondered if Lauren was the type of mom to spoil her kids at Christmas, especially their first one.

"I hope you don't mind but I invited some people over for dinner tomorrow night."

"These people have names?"

"Lauren Shayne, her mother, grandfather and twin daughters."

His mom dropped the box containing a toy ranch set, no doubt for Brent. The stunned expression on her face surprised him.

"Lauren is coming here for dinner?"

"Yeah. I thought it would be okay. If not—"

She waved off what he'd been about to say. "No, it's fine. I just…well, she's famous for her cooking."

"So are you."

"No, I'm not."

"You have no idea how many people we've all told about your chocolate cake. I'm surprised Texas hasn't been invaded by surrounding states yet for a taste."

She made a *pffftt* sound of disbelief. "Nobody would give me a TV show."

"I disagree wholeheartedly with that assumption."

"Be that as it may, I need to figure out what I'm going to cook."

"Mom, seriously, anything will be fine. They're nice, down-to-earth people."

"That right?" There was more to that question than it appeared on the surface. "Did you meet them in town just now?"

"Yes." Better to tell the truth than have her find out some other way. "I was helping Lauren wash some windows she couldn't reach when they came by."

"You seem to be helping Lauren a lot."

"I'm trying to get her business, remember?"

"And yet I've never seen you do manual labor for any other potential customers."

Damn it, she had him there. He'd never felt an attraction toward any of them, and he suspected his mom knew it.

"None of them could give us this kind of exposure."

His mom started cleaning up her wrapping station. "You go ahead and keep telling yourself it's only business."

"What's that supposed to mean?" He knew full well how her mind worked, especially since her children had started falling in love and getting married. She only had two left unattached, and since they seemed to be going in order of age he was up to the plate.

"You like that girl."

"She's nice." And his heart rate had a habit of speeding up whenever he looked at her, but he wasn't about to say that out loud. Especially since Lauren had already made it known that she wasn't relocating to Blue Falls. And after what she'd gone through with her ex, he suspected she wasn't too hot on dating anyway. Not that it kept him from wondering what it would be like.

"Uh-huh," his mom said, fully aware in that freaky way she had that he was not being totally forthcoming.

He leaned back against the table next to her. "Listen, I'm going to level with you. Yes, I like her. Yes, I think she's pretty and interesting. But you're aware of what her ex-fiancé put her through, right?"

The layer of teasing disappeared from his mom's face. "Yeah, very unfortunate."

"Then don't you think that dating is probably the last thing on her mind right now, especially since she has two babies?"

"I don't know."

He cocked an eyebrow at her. "Yes, you do. I know you're on this kick to see us all married off, and I'm not against the idea with the right person at the right time. But this isn't it."

And that fact made him feel way more disappointed than his and Lauren's short acquaintance should have.

"You never know."

"Mom, please. Just approach this as a new friendship, maybe eventually a working relationship, nothing more. Okay?"

She sighed. "Fine. I wish it was different, but I see your point."

He smiled. "I still think you should make your chocolate cake, though."

She shot him a look that said she knew good and well that he was asking for the cake for his own benefit more than anything else.

"Get out of here or I'll be serving you tapioca pudding."

He made a gagging noise. He hated tapioca. As he turned to leave, she swatted him on the behind with a roll of wrapping paper covered in cartoon reindeer, causing him to laugh.

As he headed outside to haul some hay out to the far side of the pasture, he caught himself whistling a happy tune. And he didn't think it had anything to do with the knowledge that come tomorrow night, he'd be able to dig into his mom's chocolate cake.

LAUREN PULLED INTO the ranch's driveway and asked herself for what must have been the thousandth time why she'd agreed to this dinner with the Hartley family. Not only were her feelings toward Adam oddly disconcerting, but she'd also sworn an oath to herself that she'd never mix business and personal relationships again. Not that a business relationship existed yet, and she would classify the personal side of things as budding friendship, nothing more.

Yeah, right. One did not fantasize about the sexy physical attributes of mere friends.

She once again played the refrain in her mind that just because she found him attractive didn't mean she had to act on it. Granted, being around him would be easier without the attraction, but her brain flatly refused to purge the knowledge that Adam Hartley was very pleasing to the eye. Which was only strengthened by the fact that he was friendly, helpful and got along fa- mously with her daughters.

And yet it remained that she'd been on the verge of marrying a man, spending her life with him, only to find out that everything she'd believed about him had been a lie. There was too much at stake now for her to ever allow herself to make that kind of grievous error in judgment again.

Her mom reached across and squeezed Lauren's hand. "You're thinking too much."

Lauren glanced across the car. "How could you pos- sibly know that?"

"I've been your mother for twenty-eight years. This is not a great mystery."

"Annoying."

Her mom laughed. "I'll remind you that you said that in a few years when your daughters are annoyed at you for reading them correctly."

"Seems I know someone else who was irritated by her mother knowing when she was hiding something, too," Papa Ed said from the back seat.

"Oh, hush, Dad," her mom said.

Lauren laughed, thankful for the break in the tension that had been knotted up in her middle. She was over- thinking this whole evening anyway. There were just nice people in the world who wanted to be friendly and welcoming. Evidently the Hartleys were among them. There was nothing wrong with being friends with peo- ple with whom she might eventually have a business relationship. But that was as far as it could go. It was be- yond surprising she was even having to tell herself that.

When they came within sight of the house, she had an immediate sense of welcome. The house was fronted by a long porch, where she could imagine watching the sunset across the pasture that rolled off to the west. On a chilly night like the one ahead promised to be, sitting out here wrapped in a quilt and drinking hot chocolate sounded heavenly. Though it looked completely different, she got the same sense of peace that she did at her own home overlooking the Brazos.

"This place is lovely," her mom said.

Harper piped up with what sounded like a sound of agreement from her car seat in the back.

"The stone and wood does fit in nicely with the surrounding landscape," Lauren said.

After parking, she went to remove Harper from her seat while her mom retrieved Bethany and Papa Ed unfurled himself from the back seat. He stretched and Lauren looked over at him when she heard some of his bones crack.

"Just wait," he said. "One day you'll sound like a bowl of Rice Krispies, too."

A beautiful Australian shepherd came around the back of her car, startling Lauren. She lifted Harper quickly out of reach, not knowing whether the dog would bite.

"She's harmless."

Lauren looked toward the sound of Adam's deep voice. Was it her imagination or did it sound richer, sexier, today? The sight of him in a checked shirt, jeans and a cowboy hat robbed her of speech. It was as if he got better-looking every time she saw him. More likely, her brain was malfunctioning.

Thankfully, Papa Ed bending down to pet the dog diverted her attention.

"What's her name?" Papa Ed asked.

"Maggie," Adam said, though he continued to look at Lauren for a moment longer before shifting his attention to her grandfather. "She's the official welcoming committee around here. I'm just her assistant."

Harper waved her little chubby arm in Adam's direction, as if she remembered him from their one interaction.

"Hey there, gorgeous," he said to Harper as he waved at her.

Lauren forced herself not to react to the sound of those words on Adam's lips, that for a heart-jolting second she'd imagined him saying them to her.

"Come on in," Adam said, motioning them toward the house.

As they moved that way, Lauren let her mom and grandfather go ahead, and Adam fell into step beside her. His proximity did nothing to help the jittery feeling coursing through her, making her wonder if good sense was a thing of the past.

"Mom is so excited to meet you it's been amusing to watch."

Despite her success, it still seemed so odd to Lauren that people viewed her as a celebrity.

"That's sweet, but I'm just an average person who got lucky."

"From what I hear, you're not giving yourself enough credit."

"Oh, I can cook and I work hard, but the same can be said for a lot of other people."

Adam leaned closer to her. "Maybe just let Mom have her 'meeting a celebrity' moment. The closest she's gotten before is my brother-in-law, Jason, who won the national title in steer wrestling."

She wasn't sure why that struck her as funny, but Lauren laughed. The resulting smile on Adam's face threatened to melt her resolve to not think of him in any sort of romantic light.

As they entered the house to find it filled to the gills with people, Lauren didn't know whether to be overwhelmed or thankful she had more of a buffer between her and Adam.

"Hello, hello," a woman who appeared close to her mother's age said as she crossed the room. "I'm so happy you all could make it."

"Lauren, this is my mom, Diane," Adam said, suddenly at Lauren's side again.

Whether it was because of her buzzing awareness of Adam standing near her or the sheer number of people present, she only retained about a third of the names she heard as he introduced her to his siblings, their spouses, and his nieces, nephew and parents.

"I can't get over how adorable these two are," Diane said as she allowed Harper and Bethany to each grab hold of one of her fingers.

"Thank you. I'm pretty partial to them myself."

Adam's sister Sloane wrapped her arm around her mom's shoulders. "Watch her. She hasn't met a kid she didn't try to spoil absolutely rotten."

Lauren smiled and nodded toward her mom. "She'd have some hefty competition."

"They just don't understand that it's the duty of a grandmother to spoil her grandbabies," Lauren's mom said.

"I know, right?" Diane replied.

"Can I hold the babies?" a pretty young girl asked as she looked up at Diane.

"I don't think so, honey. Go wash your hands. We're about to eat."

The girl—Julia, Angel's daughter, if Lauren was re-membering correctly—looked disappointed but did as she was told.

"She was the only child around here for several years," Diane said. "Now that she has cousins and an-other on the way, she's beside herself."

"I think she's going to take after Mom," Sloane said, "and want to keep them all."

If they hadn't been talking about a child, Lauren would have been tempted to take the twins and run. Maybe all mothers were like that, or maybe her fierce protectiveness of them was at least in part due to what she'd gone through, and that she never wanted them to be hurt in any way. Her rational brain knew they couldn't go through their entire lives without suffer-ing somehow, but it didn't erase her need to prevent it whenever she could.

"Well, dinner is ready, so everyone find a seat," Diane said, directing everyone to the dining room.

Lauren stopped short when she entered the room to find two high chairs set up next to the table.

"I still had the chair I used for Julia, and Mandy brought over Cassie's since she's sitting in a booster now," Angel said.

"That's very thoughtful," Lauren said. "Thank you."

The Hartleys had brought in an extra fold-up table and an odd assortment of chairs to seat everyone, but not a single soul seemed to mind. Lauren got the im-pression this wasn't the first time this arrangement had occurred here.

"I'm not a professional like you," Diane said as she

was the last to take her seat, "but I hope you enjoy everything."

Lauren looked along the length of the table at the wide variety and sheer amount of food filling bowls and covering platters.

"It looks and smells delicious." The same could be said for the man sitting across from her, though she wasn't about to reveal that fact to everyone.

Instead, she focused on alternating between filling her plate from the dishes being passed around and opening up jars of baby food.

When she attempted to get Bethany to eat some carrots, a new food for her, Bethany let her displeasure show by spitting the orange mess back out and screwing up her face.

"I don't blame you," Adam's brother Ben said to Bethany. "Carrots are gross."

As the conversation and laughter flowed throughout the meal, Lauren gradually relaxed. Even the twins seemed to be having a good time, but that was likely because they had a seemingly endless supply of people to tell them how cute they were and with whom they could play peekaboo.

"There is no better sound than a baby laughing," Diane said.

"I agree," Lauren said as she cleaned the mushy green beans from Harper's chin.

"So when do you think you'll open the restaurant?" Andrew, Adam's dad, asked.

"Unsure. I'd like to be open as early in the New Year as possible so we can work out any kinks before the spring wildflower season starts bringing in tourists."

Of course, it would help if little roadblocks didn't

keep popping up. She'd anticipated certain undertakings when it came to cleaning the place and ensuring it was up to code. With Adam's help, some of those smaller tasks during her first few days in Blue Falls had gone quite smoothly. But there'd been other obstacles she hadn't predicted. Like the softball-sized hole she'd found yesterday in one of the restaurant's windows overlooking the lake. Again, her first thought had been of Phil. It felt like a petty type of action she could imagine him taking. But then she'd heard a couple of other businesses in town had experienced the same problem during the overnight hours.

Andrew nodded. "Sounds like a solid plan. If you need any help, you let one of us know." He gestured toward the assembled Hartley clan with his butter knife.

"Thank you. It's kind of you to offer."

Was this family for real? Were they all this nice and helpful, or was she in the midst of a group effort to ensure she chose Rocking Horse Ranch beef for her restaurant? She really hoped it was the former, because she hated to think this many seemingly nice people could deceive her at once.

She listened as Ben told Papa Ed about his saddle-making business, then as Jason detailed the life he'd led on the rodeo circuit before retiring in favor of marriage, fatherhood and training budding steer wrestlers. It seemed a large percentage of the Hartleys had other careers besides working on the ranch.

"How did you all get into the branded-beef business?" she asked.

Adam glanced up from his plate. "Seemed like a good fit for a cattle operation."

Angel bumped her brother's shoulder with her own. "He's being too modest. Adam is our big idea guy."

"Angel," Adam said, obviously wanting her to be quiet, which of course caused Lauren's suspicion antennae to vibrate.

"What, I'm not allowed to brag about my big brother?" Angel shifted her attention to Lauren. "He's always thinking twelve steps ahead of everyone around him. Since we all have such disparate talents, he wants to brand not only the beef, but everything all of us do under the Rocking Horse Ranch name."

Lauren had seen that done successfully by another ranch in Texas, so it made sense on a business level.

"We might have eventually set up shop in the building you bought, but you beat us to the punch," Angel said.

Lauren noticed the tense look on Adam's face, as if he wished he could rewind time to stop his sister from revealing that nugget of information. She searched for some ulterior motive for him getting close to her that was somehow tied to the building he wanted, but wouldn't he want to see her fail instead of doing business with her?

When he met her gaze across the table, she saw a man searching for the right thing to say.

"It was just a thought. It wasn't anywhere near becoming reality."

He was clearly uncomfortable with the subject, which caused her mind to spin with possible reasons why. A quick glance at Angel revealed that she'd shifted her attention to her daughter. No one else seemed to be concerned about the turn of the conversation, which made Lauren wonder if she was once again looking for self-serving purpose where there wasn't any.

Some days she felt as if she needed to start seeing a therapist to work through her erosion of trust—of others and of herself. Because even though she was experiencing it and felt there were valid reasons for its existence, she also was aware enough to know it wasn't healthy or productive.

"Well, who's up for cake?" Diane asked.

Like a classroom filled with eager students who'd just been asked if they wanted an ice-cream party, hands shot up all around the table. Lauren laughed in response.

"Either this family really loves dessert or this is one tremendous cake," she said.

"Both," Adam said, appearing to have shrugged off his discomfort with the earlier topic of conversation.

"It's not Brazos Baker-level baking, but I've never had a complaint," Diane said.

The moment Lauren took her first bite of the rich chocolate cake, she realized just how much Diane had undervalued her baking skills.

"This is delicious," Lauren said. "And I promise you I'm not just saying that to be polite."

Diane beamed. "Oh, my, you've made my day."

"Mom, we've told you a million times that your cake is awesome," Sloane said.

"I know, but—"

Lauren held up a hand. "Please, don't think my opinion matters any more than anyone else's. Like I told Adam, I'm just someone who got lucky."

"And worked hard," her mother said.

"Luck is what happens when preparation meets opportunity."

Lauren couldn't believe her ears. She turned her gaze to Adam, who'd voiced the famous words by the Roman philosopher Seneca. Though she'd never once thought him stupid, the combination of Roman philosophy with hot Texas rancher wasn't something she'd ever imagined witnessing.

"That's literally my favorite quote," she said. "I have it hanging in my office at home."

He smiled a little. "Great minds, I guess."

It felt more as if the universe was attempting to tell her something, but she suspected that was just the traitorous part of her brain trying to find any and all reasons to convince her that it was safe to like this man, to trust him. The problem was she didn't trust that part of her brain.

When the meal was over, Diane flatly refused any help clearing the table or loading the dishwasher. Instead, Lauren and her family were ushered along with the rest of the gathering into the living area. There weren't enough seats for everyone, so the kids and several of the adults plopped down on the floor.

This was the perfect moment for Lauren to say they should be leaving. But before she could form the words, Adam stepped up beside her.

"You can't really see the cattle now, but would you like to see a little bit of the ranch?"

"I don't want to take the girls outside. I'm sure it's gotten chillier now that night's fallen."

"Oh, don't worry," her mom said. "Plenty of hands here to take care of them."

Lauren gave her mom a hard look, but it didn't seem to faze her. Instead, she just took Bethany from Lauren's arms. Harper was busy patting Maggie the shepherd on the head while sitting on Papa Ed's knee.

"Looks as if the babies are in good hands," Adam said.

If she protested now, she risked everyone asking why. And if the thoughts she was having about this man wouldn't go away, they at least needed to stay firmly in her own mind. She couldn't have anyone getting ideas she wasn't willing to act on.

"Okay." Not the most enthusiastic or elegant response, but it seemed to be all she could manage.

She sure hoped no one could tell how fast her heart was beating as Adam opened the door for her. She felt as if she must look like one of those old cartoon characters with her heart visibly beating out of her chest.

Thankfully, the temperature outside had dropped to the point where it cooled her warm cheeks.

"So how did work go today?" he asked as they walked toward the barn.

"Fine right up until the exterminator found evidence of termites." Which had just been the icing on the cake after the rock through the window.

"Bad?"

"Thankfully no, but it's one more thing—along with having to redo some of the wiring—that I wasn't expecting."

"Starting a business seems to be like that. Just when you think you're going along fine, some obstacle pops up in your path, one you can't just go around."

What obstacles had he faced? Did he count her not making a commitment to buy beef from his ranch one of them?

When they reached the fence next to the barn, he

pointed out across the dark rise and fall of the pasture. "Ranching is full of those kinds of things. Storms, drought, whatever Mother Nature decides to throw at you."

"Have you all had a lot of those kinds of problems?" Her suspicious side wondered if this conversation was aimed at generating sympathy.

He shrugged. "No more than pretty much every other rancher. It's just the nature of the business."

She glanced at his profile in the dim light. Even without full illumination, he was a handsome man.

"Is that why you came up with the branding plan Angel was talking about?"

He leaned his forearms against the top of the fence and stared out into the darkness. "I wish she hadn't mentioned that."

"Why?"

"Because they're just ideas at this point, might be all they ever are."

"Now that doesn't sound like you." How odd that she knew that about him after so brief an acquaintance.

He looked over at her. "What makes you say that?"

"You just seem like you're driven. I mean, you were willing to move furniture just so I'd listen to your sales pitch."

"That's not all it was."

An electric buzzing launched along her nerves. What did he mean by that?

A sudden gust of wind seemed to drop the temperature by several degrees, causing her to shiver.

"Here," Adam said as he pulled off his jacket and wrapped it around her shoulders before she could voice a protest.

The instant warmth that was a product of his body hit her in the same moment as his scent—earthy but clean, as if his shower could never fully wash away the pleasant smell of the outdoors. Without considering how close he still stood, she looked up to thank him. And promptly forgot what she was going to say. Forgot what words even were.

Chapter Seven

He couldn't kiss her. No matter how much the need to do exactly that thrummed within him. He knew he should look away, remove his hands from where they held the lapels of the jacket he'd just draped around her shoulders. But he felt frozen in the moment, unwilling to let it thaw quite yet.

"You didn't have to do that," she said, her voice not sounding quite normal.

"I'm fine." When he wondered how she might react if he lowered his lips to hers, it somehow gave him the push he needed to step away. "It'll be warmer inside the barn."

He watched as she glanced toward the house before giving him a quick nod. When he looked away from her toward the barn door, his breath came rushing back into his lungs. It took some effort to remind himself that he shouldn't jeopardize a possible lucrative business relationship by kissing a woman who most likely didn't want to be kissed. If he'd been betrayed like she had been, he doubted he'd want anything to do with a woman for a good long time.

He flicked on the lights as soon as he stepped inside then closed the door behind Lauren to keep out the wind. She started to shrug out of his jacket, so he lightly touched her arm.

"You keep it. I'm really okay."

"I didn't think to bring one. I suppose I should pay more attention to the forecast." No doubt she hadn't had room in her brain for thoughts of the weather because too much had been occupied with nervous anticipation about seeing Adam again.

"Yeah, the weather can be moody this time of year."

Needing some distance between them, she walked over to a dappled gray horse and let him sniff her fingers. She desperately needed something to keep her mind off the words Adam had spoken before he'd wrapped her in his jacket.

That's not all it was.

What had he meant by that? Was she reading too much into a statement that only meant he'd been trying to be nice? Neighborly? She had to find a way to not think everyone had ulterior motives or life was going to be miserable.

Forcing down any hint of the attraction she felt toward him, she turned to face Adam. "So tell me about the plans Angel mentioned."

He leaned against the stall across from her. "Why do you want to know?"

She shrugged. "Curious. You know how they call people who love politics policy wonks? Well, I'm a bit of a business wonk. I've always been interested in how people find creative ways to make money, especially doing stuff they love. Some kids had lemonade stands. I made little decorated cupcakes when I was a kid and sold them on the playground, on the school bus."

He smiled. "I can just imagine."

"Were you always the same?"

He shook his head and averted his eyes, looking down the length of the barn. "I was a pretty normal kid, both before and after my parents died. But when your livelihood depends on so many factors out of your control, there can be lean years. I saw that not long after Mom and Dad adopted me. One stroke of bad luck you can weather, even if it's hard, but two years in a row brings you to the breaking point. It affected all of us kids, and now we're all determined to make sure we're never that close to losing the ranch again."

His story struck a familiar chord in Lauren's heart, in her memory, and she was thankful he wasn't looking at her or he might see the tears that she quickly blinked away.

"Thing is I don't have a talent like Angel does with photography or Ben does with leather-working. Neil is so much like Dad and following in his footsteps that you'd never know they weren't related by blood. Even Sloane has found a way to increase the ranch's name recognition through philanthropy."

"So the beef operation and the idea for the branded merchandise is your contribution."

He returned his gaze to her. "That's the idea." He pointed toward his temple. "What goes through my head over and over is that it could ensure the ranch not only survives as a family-owned operation, but thrives. There's a new generation now, and I want the ranch to be safe for them as they grow up."

Did he envision that new generation including children of his own? He certainly didn't sound like a guy who would abandon his own children.

But that was totally different to being willing to

be a father to children who weren't his. She mentally smacked herself. Could she really imagine him thinking that way when he and his siblings were raised by parents that they'd not been born to?

And why was she even thinking those kinds of thoughts anyway?

"It sounds like a good idea to me," she said.

"Thanks. I just have to be more patient. I get these ideas and wish I could make them a reality overnight."

She laughed a little. "Not how it works." She wandered over to a stack of hay bales and sat down. "People sometimes look at me and think I'm an overnight success, but that couldn't be further from the truth. It's taken years, countless hours of worry and hard work and sleep deprivation to get to this point. And if I'm being honest, I still think I'll make a mistake and lose it all."

Adam crossed to where she was sitting—slowly, as if giving her time to move if she felt crowded—and sat beside her.

"Is that what you're thinking about the restaurant now? If you don't mind me saying, you seem a bit tense and distracted."

Oh, if he only knew what the main reason for that was at this moment.

"Yeah. It's a big investment, and having it so far from where I live… I guess I'll question the decision until the place is a success."

"It will be."

She glanced over at him, wishing that for a few minutes she was free of any and all concerns about giving in to her attraction. "What makes you so certain?"

"Your determination and the fact you've been a success at every other aspect of your business. That can't just be by chance." He smiled and her heart thumped a bit harder. "I bet even your elementary-school cupcake business was a success."

There was something about Adam that made her want to be open and honest with him, and that scared her. And yet she found herself speaking a truth she didn't share with many people.

"It helped." At his curious expression, she continued. "You said your family went through tough times. Mine did, too, after my dad died. Mom had just been a volunteer aide at my school, but after Dad's accident she went to work full-time at a convenience store. At the same time, she got her teaching degree. My sister and I spent a lot of time at Papa Ed and Nana Gloria's. Nana was the one who taught me how to bake."

"She's gone now?" The tone of Adam's voice was kind, understanding, and she realized there must have been something in the way she said Nana Gloria's name that had revealed the truth.

Lauren nodded. "She passed about a year ago."

"I'm sorry."

"It's honestly why I agreed to visit Blue Falls in the first place. I wanted to do something fun with Papa Ed, and he suggested a trip back to his boyhood home. I had no idea he had something up his sleeve until we were at an empty restaurant building and a real estate agent showed up. I'll admit I was a little worried he was losing it when he suggested I buy the building here."

"But you obviously came around to the idea."

"Nobody was more surprised than I was when I walked inside and it was perfect." She noticed how Adam looked down at the ground between his boots. "I'm sorry it was the place you had your eye on."

"No need to apologize. I mean, it's been sitting there empty for a while."

"Still."

"My mom always says that things turn out how they're supposed to."

"I really like your mom," Lauren said.

"Your family is nice, too. And they obviously think your girls hung the moon."

"You have no idea. If I'm not careful between them and, admittedly, myself, the twins are going to be spoiled rotten to the core." She realized she was probably overcompensating for the fact they were going to grow up without a father in their lives.

"I think it's natural to want to give kids a better life than we had at their age."

She didn't just glance at Adam this time. She openly stared.

"What?" he asked when he noticed.

"You're very perceptive."

"My sisters would disagree with you."

"No, really." She paused, unable to look away from him. It might be dangerous, might be foolish, but she trusted him. "The reason I made those cupcakes and sold them when I was a kid was because I wanted to help my mom pay the bills. I was young but I still saw the worry on her face. I don't want my girls to ever have to experience that. I don't want any of my family to ever have to be concerned about money ever again."

"Sounds as if we're in the same boat."

She had an image of floating along the lake's surface with him in a little boat, much like Rapunzel and Flynn in *Tangled*. She had the same butterfly-wings feeling in her chest now as she'd imagined those two characters felt during that scene.

Logically she knew it was only mere moments, but the time that passed as they stared at each other seemed much longer. When Adam's gaze dropped momentarily to her lips, part of Lauren urged her to lean in and give him permission. But a memory of the last time she'd kissed a man shoved its way to the front of her brain, causing her to look away so quickly it bordered on rude.

"I should be going. Won't be long before I need to get the girls to bed. Hopefully they'll sleep better tonight." She stood and took a few steps away from him.

"If you want a place with more privacy, where you don't have to worry about the girls' crying waking other guests, you should check out the cabins at the Vista Hills Guest Ranch."

"Maybe I will. Thanks."

When he stood, she started to slip out of his jacket again.

"Wait until we get back to the house."

"I won't freeze between here and there."

He smiled. "Neither will I."

As they left the barn, she had to admit she was thankful for the extra layer of protection his jacket provided. The only sounds she heard as they crossed the darker area between the barn and house were the crunch of the gravel under their feet and the call of some night bird she couldn't identify. When they neared the porch, Adam slowed, causing her to do the same, and then she stopped when he did.

He appeared on the verge of asking her something, and her breath caught in her throat—half in anticipation, half in fear. But she saw him change what he'd been about to say as surely as if she'd seen him change hats.

"I hope you all had a nice time tonight."

"Uh, we did. Thank you for inviting us."

"The offer stands to come out and tour the operation when you can actually see something."

She realized it was the first time since her arrival at the ranch that he'd directly addressed their potential working relationship.

"When I get a chance."

He nodded. Again, she thought he had something else to say, but instead he simply escorted her up the front steps.

She was so occupied with wondering what he'd been going to say that she forgot to remove his jacket until she'd already stepped through the front door. Though she was likely imagining things, it felt as if every set of eyes in the room noticed and immediately started assigning deeper meaning to Adam's kind gesture.

Sure, she wasn't entirely sure there wasn't some unspoken meaning, but no one else needed to know that. So she deliberately made eye contact with Adam as she slipped out of the jacket and handed it back to him.

"Thanks." Then before he could respond, she turned toward her mom. "It's gotten quite chilly out there. We need to make sure to wrap up the girls really well."

With so many people present, it was impossible to make a quick exit. But the flurry of goodbyes did give her time to calm herself a bit before she found herself on the porch with Adam for the final farewell of the night.

"Thanks again for dinner. It was nice to meet everyone and have such a good meal."

"Well, you made my mom's night. Possibly her year."

She imagined him leaning down to kiss her good-night, found herself wanting that even if it was a peck on the cheek. Which was her cue to leave.

As she drove back toward Blue Falls a few minutes later, she couldn't stop thinking about that moment in the yard when she'd swear he'd been about to say something entirely different to her. She had a feeling that question was much more likely to keep her awake tonight than cranky babies.

ADAM WAS THANKFUL for the late-night storm that had blown through. It gave him an excuse to go ride around the ranch the next day to check on the fencing and the cattle. He needed the time away from his mom's curious gaze. She hadn't questioned him or even made any comments alluding to the time he'd spent outside with Lauren the night before, or the fact Lauren had come back to the house wearing his jacket, but that didn't mean he couldn't see the curiosity, and probably hope, in his mom's eyes.

Despite his determination not to jeopardize the possible contract with her restaurant, he'd almost asked her out. With one question, he could have torpedoed the deal. Maybe even his business if word got out he'd been denied by the famous Brazos Baker in favor of another supplier.

But what if he could land another large account? Would that give him the freedom to ask her out to dinner?

He shook his head as he rode over a rise in the land that gave one of the prettiest panoramic views on the ranch. He reined his horse to a stop and soaked in the sight before him. This was what he was working to protect, ensuring that it stayed in the Hartley family no matter what Mother Nature or the temperamental economy threw at them.

Adam inhaled deeply of the fresh, rain-scented air, always good for clearing his mind. Though Lauren had shared personal details with him the night before, that didn't mean she was interested in him the way he was in her. He reminded himself she had good reason.

And yet there'd been that moment when she'd looked up at him as he'd wrapped his jacket around her shoulders. Had he read it so wrong? Because he would have sworn he saw interest on her part, as well.

Maybe she'd just been startled by his action. But she'd been willing to sit beside him inside the barn and talk about the tough years they'd both experienced as kids. That, however, was something friends would do, not necessarily more than friends.

He rubbed his hand over his face and rode on. But try as he might to think about other things, his thoughts kept coming back to Lauren. What was it about her that drew him so much? Yes, she was beautiful, but she wasn't the only beautiful woman in the world. Not even the only one in Blue Falls. There was more to it, something that pulled at him on a deeper level, though for the life of him he couldn't identify what.

When he saw her again, he had to remember, however, that it wasn't just the potential business deal that should keep him from voicing his feelings. She'd been through a lot, and maybe memories of the past were what caused the nervousness he sometimes sensed she felt around him. Maybe the best thing now was to keep his distance, only occasionally check in with a professional call.

Dear Reader,

IT'S A FACT: if you answer 4 quick questions, we'll send you **4 FREE REWARDS!**

I'm not kidding you. As a leading publisher of women's fiction, we value your opinions... and your time. That's why we are prepared to **reward** you handsomely for completing our mini-survey. In fact, we have 4 Free Rewards for you, including 2 free books and 2 free gifts.

As you may have guessed, that's why our mini-survey is called **"4 for 4"**. Answer 4 questions and get 4 Free Rewards. It's that simple!

Thank you for participating in our survey,

Pam Powers

To get your 4 FREE REWARDS:
Complete the survey below and return the insert today to receive 2 FREE BOOKS and 2 FREE GIFTS guaranteed!

"4 for 4" MINI-SURVEY

1 Is reading one of your favorite hobbies?
☐ YES ☐ NO

2 Do you prefer to read instead of watch TV?
☐ YES ☐ NO

3 Do you read newspapers and magazines?
☐ YES ☐ NO

4 Do you enjoy trying new book series with FREE BOOKS?
☐ YES ☐ NO

YES! I have completed the above Mini-Survey. Please send me my 4 FREE REWARDS (worth over $20 retail). I understand that I am under no obligation to buy anything, as explained on the back of this card.

235/335 HDL GMYE

FIRST NAME	LAST NAME

ADDRESS

APT.#	CITY

STATE/PROV.	ZIP/POSTAL CODE

READER SERVICE—Here's how it works:

Accepting your 2 free Harlequin® Special Edition books and 2 free gifts (gifts valued at approximately $10.00 retail) places you under no obligation to buy anything. You may keep the books and gifts and return the shipping statement marked "cancel." If you do not cancel, about a month later we'll send you 6 additional books and bill you just $4.99 each in the U.S. or $5.74 each in Canada. That is a savings of at least 12% off the cover price. It's quite a bargain! Shipping and handling is just 50¢ per book in the U.S. and 75¢ per book in Canada*. You may cancel at any time, but if you choose to continue, every month we'll send you 6 more books, which you may either purchase at the discount price plus shipping and handling or return to us and cancel your subscription. *Terms and prices subject to change without notice. Prices do not include applicable taxes. Sales tax applicable in N.Y. Canadian residents will be charged applicable taxes. Offer not valid in Quebec. Books received may not be as shown. All orders subject to approval. Credit or debit balances in a customer's account(s) may be offset by any other outstanding balance owed by or to the customer. Please allow 4 to 6 weeks for delivery. Offer available while quantities last.

▲ If offer card is missing write to: Reader Service, P.O. Box 1341, Buffalo, NY 14240-8531 or visit www.ReaderService.com ▲

BUSINESS REPLY MAIL

FIRST-CLASS MAIL   PERMIT NO. 717   BUFFALO, NY

POSTAGE WILL BE PAID BY ADDRESSEE

READER SERVICE
PO BOX 1341
BUFFALO NY 14240-8571

NO POSTAGE
NECESSARY
IF MAILED
IN THE
UNITED STATES

His phone dinged with a text, pulling him from his mental meandering. He slipped the phone from his jacket pocket and a jolt of excitement went through him at the sight of Lauren's name on the display. So much for shoving her from his mind.

He tapped the screen to read the message.

Got any recommendations for a roofer?

Okay, so that wasn't exactly the kind of message he imagined getting from her, but at least it wasn't radio silence. He hadn't scared her off completely.

He texted back a couple of suggestions, then like some sort of lovesick teenager, he stared at his phone until she texted back a simple Thanks. He blew out a breath and headed on toward the southern property boundary.

It was a good thing mind reading wasn't actually a thing because he still hadn't been able to stop thinking about Lauren when he returned to the house late in the afternoon. His brain refused to stop running possible scenarios in which he could preserve the chance to do business with her while also exploring his attraction.

As he left the barn and headed toward the house, he met Arden, Neil's wife, leaving. He remembered then that she'd had a prenatal checkup that morning.

"Hey, how are things going with the little peanut?"

She smiled and placed her hand against her still-flat stomach. "Good. Though I thought your brother was going to pass out he was so nervous. I can't imagine what he'll be like when I actually go in to have the baby."

Adam laughed. "You are the best sister-in-law ever for telling me that. Just don't tell Mandy I said so."

They started to go their separate ways again.

"Adam?"

He turned back toward Arden. "Yeah?"

"Can I ask you something?"

"Sure."

"Is it my imagination or are you interested in Lauren?"

Ah, hell. "She's nice, and I'm hoping we can land her restaurant as a customer."

Arden crossed her arms and gave him an incredulous look he imagined she'd used to great effect with tough interviewees during her years as an international reporter.

"You know that's not what I mean."

He sighed. There was no use lying to someone who'd literally gone to war-torn areas of the globe and gotten the truth out of people who didn't like telling the truth.

"Yes, but I can't do anything about it."

"Why not?"

He retraced his steps and leaned against the side of Arden's car. "Do you know anything about what she's been through?"

"A bit."

He filled in the gaps, and when he was finished, his brother's wife leaned back against the car beside him.

"So you're afraid that she's gun-shy."

He nodded.

She was quiet for a few seconds before speaking again. "It's kind of you to put her feelings first, but she hasn't actually told you she's not interested, has she?"

"No, but I haven't asked, either."

"Then maybe you should."

"I don't want to jeopardize the potential business deal. We need a big win."

"I understand. But I don't want you to miss something that could be way more important."

"How can I tell if she's interested or if I should keep my distance because of what she's been through?"

"Don't come on too strong. One little step at a time. And honestly, she might not be receptive at first. The hurt might be too fresh in her memory. But take it from me, sometimes people don't know what they need until someone shows them."

He knew she was talking about how Neil had initially offered her friendship after she'd come home from being a captive of human traffickers in Africa, and how that friendship had slowly built into something more that neither of them had expected. And now Adam couldn't imagine two people more in love.

He didn't know if anything even remotely similar was in store for him and Lauren. Him and anyone, for that matter. But Arden was right. He wasn't going to find out if he avoided Lauren, if he let his fear of failure keep him from figuring out if their new friendship might eventually grow into something more.

Chapter Eight

A cold wind blew off the lake into downtown Blue Falls, making it feel like the perfect weather to do some Christmas shopping. Add in the fact that the restaurant was unbearably noisy at the moment with the roofers doing the needed repairs, and Lauren decided to use the time wisely. Her mom had returned home and to her classroom, but Papa Ed was still on babysitting duty.

Lauren had been so busy lately that she hadn't given the holiday season much thought. But as she strolled down the sidewalk and saw the storefront windows filled with Christmas displays, and as she hummed along with the familiar carols playing on outdoor speakers the length of the Main Street shopping district, she felt the holiday spirit bubble up within her.

At each shop she entered, she was greeted with warmth and enthusiasm. Inevitably people wanted to know when she'd be opening for business, and she would always say the same thing—that she hoped to be open by spring. She still thought she could make that goal if unexpected repairs didn't keep popping up, along with their accompanying price tags. Despite the setbacks, she wasn't about to skimp on Christmas. After everything her family had been through the past couple of years, they all deserved a big, beautiful, happy holiday season.

By the time she reached A Good Yarn, she was toting several bags filled with gifts. The moment she stepped inside the store, she felt as if her first breath inhaled Christmas itself. The delicious scents of cinnamon, clove and nutmeg with a hint of pine filled the air and "Let it Snow" by Dean Martin reminded her of her family's tradition of spending Christmas Eve watching old black-and-white Christmas movies. Everything from classics like *Miracle on 34th Street* to lesser-known films such as *The Shop Around the Corner*, which many people didn't realize was the inspiration for *You've Got Mail*.

"Can I help you?" a pretty woman with curly waves of red hair asked as she emerged from the center aisle.

"It feels so much like Christmas in here I feel as if it might start snowing."

The woman laughed. "Well, that would certainly get the shop on the front page of the paper."

"Lauren, I thought that sounded like you." Mandy Hartley appeared from the back of the store, causing Lauren to remember one of the family facts she'd learned during her dinner with the Hartley family. Mandy was part owner of this store.

Mandy came forward and pulled Lauren into a hug as if they'd known each other for ages, then turned toward the other woman.

"This is Lauren Shayne."

"Oh, the baker I've heard so much about. Nice to meet you."

"You, too."

"Sorry," Mandy said. "This is Devon Davis, my best

friend and the person who started all this." She gestured toward their surroundings.

"Can I stow your shopping bags for you while you look around?" Devon asked.

"Thanks. That would be great. I may have gone a little overboard."

Devon smiled as she accepted the bags. "Feel free to continue to do so."

Lauren smiled, already able to tell she liked Mandy's business partner.

As Devon walked behind the front counter, Mandy asked, "Is there something I can help you find?"

"Do you have lavender-scented candles? My mom loves them."

"Yes, we do." Mandy motioned for Lauren to follow her.

On a large wooden shelving unit along one wall of the store was a display of seemingly every size and scent of candle anyone could ever want.

"Wow."

Mandy smiled. "Yeah, we feature candles from a few different area artisans. Same with a lot of the other products we have."

"I have the oddest desire to take up knitting while enjoying the scent of vanilla candles."

"Well, we can hook you up."

"Hey, I'm going to run to the bakery," Devon called from the front of the store. "Either of you want anything?"

"A hot chocolate sounds nice." Mandy looked at Lauren. "Want one?"

"I don't want to be any trouble."

Mandy waved off Lauren's concern while making a dismissive sound. "Make that two."

"That's taking customer service to a new level," Lauren said as she picked up a large jar containing a lavender candle.

"Small town. And this time of year puts us in a good mood."

"I've got to admit that Blue Falls feels a bit like one of those quintessential small towns in a holiday movie. Everyone is so friendly."

"It has a few stinkers like anywhere else, but overall it's a great place to live and work."

The front door opened, though it was too soon for Devon to be back.

"Look around and if I can help you with anything else, just let me know." Mandy headed toward the front of the store to greet the new arrivals.

The store was so cozy and appealing that Lauren took her time browsing, partly because she didn't want to miss anything and partly because she had a feeling she'd get some good ideas for creating atmosphere for her own gift shop. By the time she wandered back up to the front of the building, she'd put not only the candles for her mom in a basket, but also two large vanilla ones to burn at the restaurant while she was working, some goat milk soaps that smelled heavenly and two little knitted hats for the twins. She also carried a striking painting of a field of wildflowers that she could already envision gracing the entrance to her restaurant.

Even more customers had entered the store, claiming Mandy's attention. It must be just as busy at the bakery because Devon hadn't yet returned. But for once, Lauren wasn't in a hurry. She didn't often allow herself time to just be alone to do whatever she wanted, but the incessant hammering of roofers gave her the perfect excuse. That and the fact Christmas was likely to sneak up on her front steps and pound on the door, demanding to be let in, before she was ready.

Though she didn't knit, she let her gaze drift across the skeins of brightly colored yarn stacked in wooden cubbies along the wall opposite the wall of candles. The woolen rainbow could be seen from outside, which she was certain was by design, aiming to lure inside anyone who'd ever even had a passing thought about knitting.

She glanced past the lovely Christmas display in the window and spotted Adam across the street. He was talking to a man she didn't recognize. Since he was unaware of her gaze upon him, she didn't immediately look away. Instead, she took her first opportunity to simply look at him. Though he wore a tan cowboy hat, she could see the ends of his dark hair curling at the bottom edges. For that unobserved moment, she imagined what it might be like to run her fingers through it. Was the texture soft or coarse? Would he respond in kind, threading his fingers through the length of her hair, as well?

"Like the view?"

Lauren jumped and let loose a little yelp of surprise. So much for being unobserved.

"Was just watching for the hot-chocolate delivery."

"So this has nothing to do with the fact that my brother-in-law is standing across the street?"

"Who?" Seriously, did she just try to pretend she hadn't seen Adam even though she'd been caught staring straight at him. "Oh, Adam. Who is that he's talking to?"

"Adrian Stone, local attorney."

An attorney? A chill ran down her back. Why would he have reason to talk with an attorney? Did this have something to do with the ranch? His plans to open a mercantile?

Or maybe it's a small town and people just know each other.

When she dared a glance at Mandy, Lauren could tell the other woman had picked up on her interest in Adam. But that didn't mean Lauren was going to verify it in any shape or form. And whether Mandy read something on her face or she knew about what had gone down with Phil and decided not to press the point, Mandy didn't pursue the topic of her brother-in-law any further. Instead, she pointed at the basket Lauren held.

"Looks as if you took Devon's advice and found plenty of things to buy."

"It was amazingly easy."

"That's what we like to hear."

Just then Devon returned with a cup carrier and white bag in tow.

"Wow, the bakery is full today," Devon said as she placed her purchases atop the round table surrounded by comfy chairs in the corner opposite the checkout counter. "Seems word has gotten out that Keri is giving away a free cookie—a new flavor—with every beverage purchase."

"Please tell me that's what is in the bag," Mandy said.

"Of course. Do you think I'd refuse free cookies?" Devon pulled out three cookies in paper sleeves and handed one to Mandy and one to Lauren. "Salted caramel sugar cookies."

Lauren's mouth watered and when she took a bite she

shut her eyes as the flavors danced across her tongue. At the sounds of appreciation from the other women, she opened her eyes.

"I think I might have chosen to go into business in the wrong community."

"Nonsense," Mandy said. "We need a good barbecue place. I think it's actually against the law for a town in Texas not to have one."

Lauren waited for Mandy to say something about the Rocking Horse Ranch providing the necessary beef for said barbecue, but she didn't. Maybe she was just too busy enjoying what Lauren had to admit was an excellent cookie.

"Tell you what might be interesting, though," Mandy said. "There's a Christmas carnival coming up soon at the elementary school, and one of the booths is going to be a cakewalk. Keri always donates at least one cake. Maybe you could make one, too? We could bill it as 'Battle of the Bakers' and draw a nice crowd."

"I don't think antagonizing the long-established local baker is a good business move."

Mandy and Devon snickered.

"Are you kidding?" Devon said. "Keri will eat it up with a spoon. The people who donate cakes regularly help run the booth, and there is good-natured heckling of each other."

"Plus the money is a big fund-raiser for the local schools," Mandy added. "This year the funds are going to buy new science textbooks and drums for the band."

"Well, I can't really say no to that, can I?"

"Awesome." Mandy sure did look as if she was happy about Lauren taking part in the carnival.

Lauren was afraid it had less to do with the good of

the school and more to do with Adam. If Blue Falls was like most small towns, activities at the schools drew at least half the population.

As Lauren left with her purchases a few minutes later, she had a hard time not fantasizing about Adam winning her cake in the musical-chairs style game and proclaiming it the best thing he'd ever eaten. Thank goodness he no longer stood across the street or she was certain he'd see the truth written on her face.

LAUREN HAD BEEN right about half the town showing up for the Christmas carnival. The gym was so filled with people browsing the craft booths, waiting in line for hot dogs and giant soft pretzels, and playing a wide array of games for prizes that it was a challenge to weave her way through the crowd without dropping or having someone knock the seven-layer spice cake with cream-cheese icing from her hands. Though if it did topple, maybe she could salvage enough to eat herself. Her mouth had watered when she'd pulled it out of the oven that morning.

Baking back in the familiar warmth of her own kitchen had been wonderful, but she'd also found herself anxious to return to Blue Falls at the same time. She knew that had a good bit to do with the fact that she expected to see Adam tonight. It didn't seem to matter how often she told herself the attraction she felt toward him could go no further than daydreams, she continued to think of him way too often.

Evidently she mentioned him too often as well because her sister had picked up on it and felt it necessary to point it out.

"Is there anyone else who lives in Blue Falls?" Violet

had asked as they'd cleaned up after the Thanksgiving meal at their mom's house a few days ago.

"What?"

Violet grinned in that playfully wicked way she had. "I should have started a tally chart to see how many times you mentioned Adam Hartley's name."

"You're exaggerating."

"Am I?"

"He's just helped me out a bit. And he has a vested interest."

"Do you really think he's doing all these things to help just so you'll do business with him?"

Her instinct told her no, but how could she be certain? She also suspected if she said no, Violet was going to read way more into his actions than was there.

"It wouldn't be the first time a man has fooled me, would it?"

Violet's gaze darkened. "I can't tell you how many times I've wanted to go find Phil and slap him right off the continent."

"Line forms behind me." Not surprisingly, Phil's child-support payment was missing in action. Of course, so was he.

Thankfully she was in a position to provide whatever her daughters needed. She felt angry on behalf of all the women who weren't as financially stable as she was and still had to deal with deadbeat dads.

Two little boys, each with a handful of game tickets, barreled past Lauren, bringing her back to the present in time to lift her cake up to a safe height. Behind her, Violet squealed and nearly dropped the raspberry strudel she'd made. Her sister had the ability to bake some tasty treats herself when she put her mind to it.

"I feel as if I'm on one of those obstacle-course shows," Violet said.

"Almost there." Ahead she spied the rather elaborately decorated cakewalk area crowned with, no joke, a curved sign that said Battle of the Bakers over the entrance to the cordoned-off, numbered-spaces area for the walkers. She also spotted Mandy, India Parrish, who owned the Yesterwear Boutique, and Keri Teague chatting next to the table already filling up with cakes.

"Hey!" Mandy said and waved when she spotted Lauren. "Glad you made it. I've had probably three dozen people ask me if your cake was here yet." She glanced at Keri. "Inquiries have been neck and neck for you two."

"I'm sure it has nothing to do with the 'Battle of the Bakers' sign," Lauren said.

Mandy smiled. "Remember, it's a good cause."

"Well, here's my contribution to the cause, then." Lauren extended her cake.

"Great, what kind is it?"

"Seven-layer spice with cream-cheese icing."

"Mmm, sounds delicious. Going to be a hard call between this and Keri's gorgeous red velvet cake." Mandy nodded toward what was, indeed, a cake so pretty you wouldn't want to make the first cut.

"Well, I'm only famous adjacent, but here's a raspberry strudel."

"This is my sister, Violet," Lauren said.

Mandy accepted the strudel and extended her hand. "Very nice to meet you."

Lauren made all the introductions as more cakes arrived and attendees made inquiries about when the cakewalk was going to begin.

"In about five minutes," Mandy said. "We have the cakes divided into different rounds."

When the people inquiring left, Mandy turned back toward Lauren and the rest of their little group. "We decided to put your cakes in the last round to build up the suspense." She smiled. "Feel free to take your time showing the twins around the carnival until then."

"Where are those beautiful babies of yours?" Keri asked.

"Our grandfather has them in the stroller out in the lobby. Hard to make it quickly across a crowd this size when everyone wants to admire not one but two babies."

True to her word, Mandy started the cakewalk five minutes later. Lauren got drawn into talking to fans of her show and signing autographs. Even though her cake wasn't up for a prize in the earlier rounds, she convinced several people to go ahead and take part because there were a lot of yummy-looking cakes available. And it was true. Not one of the cakes spread out along the tables looked unappetizing. Even the two store-bought cakes looked good. Granted, she was hungry, but they did look moist and very, very chocolatey, a good combination in her opinion.

It was a good fifteen to twenty minutes before Papa Ed made it to the cakewalk area. Bethany was batting at a yellow helium balloon while Harper examined her little pink terry-cloth bunny as if she'd never seen it before. Some kids had security blankets. Harper had a security bunny.

"There are my girls," Lauren said as she crouched in front of them and played with their little sock-clad toes.

"They've sure been a hit," Papa Ed said, obviously proud to have been able to show them off.

"So has their mom," Violet said. "We may have a cake riot before the night is out."

"Don't be ridiculous." Lauren shook her head. Sure, the people she'd met seemed enthusiastic and she never minded talking to fans, but there was still a part of her that was uncomfortable with being put on any kind of pedestal, even imaginary. She probably always would be. She had to admit that part of her was jealous of Keri, who enjoyed the accolades for her baking and owned a successful business, but who wasn't so exposed. Her relationships and betrayals weren't played out before the public eye.

Though no one had mentioned anything about Phil tonight, had they? Another point in the favor of the residents of Blue Falls.

The music for the cakewalk ended and Mandy called out the winning number. The woman who'd won went immediately to Violet's strudel, which made Violet smile and do a little dance. Lauren couldn't help but laugh at her sister's antics.

"Watch out, sis," Violet called out. "I'm hot on your heels."

As the evening progressed, Lauren saw several more members of the Hartley family. All except the one she hoped to see. Maybe his absence was a sign from the universe, one she should have the good sense to heed. One she shouldn't need in the first place.

Then why did she feel so disheartened?

It was just the season. Christmas was always a tough time of year when you didn't have, or had lost, a significant other. She'd already been through one such holiday season since her breakup with Phil. How quickly she forgot.

"So I hear this is where the action is."

Lauren's pulse jumped at the sound of Adam's voice. It was thrilling and scary at the same time that she could recognize his voice without seeing him. She'd swear it vibrated something within her that she'd feared had been torched to nonexistence by how Phil had treated her.

"It is indeed," Lauren said as she turned to face him.

Mandy called out that the final grouping of cakes was now up for grabs. Several people who'd been lingering around waiting for this moment surged forward onto the numbered spaces.

"Looks as if I'm just in time," Adam said as he held up one red ticket.

"Yes, Keri's red velvet cake looks delicious."

Adam smiled as he stepped onto the last available space. "It's not her cake I intend to win."

There was something new in Adam's eyes tonight, some mixture of determination and… She didn't dare name what else she thought she might see, afraid if she did she'd want it more than she should.

They broke eye contact when the music started.

"I see now why you talk about him so much," Violet said as she came to stand next to Lauren and bumped her shoulder with her own. "He's capital *H-O-T*."

Yes, he was. And she was afraid she wanted him to win her cake more than she had wanted anything in a very long time.

Chapter Nine

Adam still wasn't sure his decision to make known his interest in Lauren the person, and not just Lauren the business owner, was the right one. He was making a big gamble, in more ways than one. But his conversation with Arden had stuck with him, making him look at the situation from a different angle. He still wasn't going to push Lauren or give her any reason to doubt him, but he couldn't ignore that he thought about her way more than a passing acquaintance would warrant.

And he trusted Arden. She'd been through a type of hell he'd never wish on anyone, and she'd come back to Blue Falls a broken version of herself. But Neil's friendship and support, based partly on his own experience with trauma, had helped her regain her strength—both physically and mentally—and their friendship had grown into love.

He didn't know if that's what lay ahead for him and Lauren, but he wanted to find out. Arden had suggested he go slowly but to be honest at the same time.

And so he was here feeling admittedly a little silly trying to win her cake. He had to land on the winning number because there was no doubt in his mind that whoever did was going to choose the cake by the famous Brazos Baker.

He glanced over to where she stood with another woman, who looked a good deal like her. Must be her sister, Violet.

The music stopped so suddenly that he nearly bumped into the woman in front of him.

"Number eleven is the lucky winner," Mandy called out.

He looked down and saw that he stood on number seven. Damn. Maybe he should have bribed his sister-in-law to allow him to win.

The kid standing on the winning spot hurried to the table and chose a tray of cupcakes decorated with superheroes. Unbelievably Adam had another chance. But his excitement dimmed when none other than Tim Wainwright stepped onto the spot vacated by the winner.

Adam's jaw clenched. Tim couldn't win Lauren's cake. The man already had enough going for him, and the memory of seeing him dancing with Lauren raked across Adam's nerves like coarse sandpaper.

"Good luck, everyone," Mandy called out as she started the music again. She looked at Adam, and he could see in her eyes that she was pulling for him. Especially considering one part of his competition.

He made eye contact with Lauren as he walked the circle. She offered a small smile, and he liked to think that maybe she was rooting for him, as well. Of course, it wouldn't matter if the entire gym full of people were on his side, it would all come down to the luck of the draw.

The music seemed to go on forever. When it finally stopped and Mandy identified five as the winner, Adam pressed his lips together to keep from cursing. Wainwright stood on the winning number. And he went right to Lauren's cake.

Feeling like a fool, Adam started to step out of the circle. But before he could, Violet stepped up next to him.

"Give me one of your tickets," she said.

"What?"

"Hurry, before the music starts again."

He did as requested then watched as Violet strode back to where Tim was talking to Lauren, probably trying to convince her that his winning her cake was some sort of sign she should have dinner with him. Adam damn near growled like a bear about to charge. Violet wrapped her arm around her sister's, said something brief and led Lauren toward the circle. Lauren looked startled by her sister's actions, but the disappointed look on Tim's face made Adam's day.

As soon as Lauren stepped onto her spot, Mandy started the music. This time, the round seemed to go quickly, but then Adam spent the entire time watching Lauren up ahead of him while trying to appear as if he wasn't.

When the music stopped yet again and Mandy announced the winning number, Adam glanced down to find he'd finally landed on the right spot. Maybe this was still salvageable. He crossed to the table and spotted Keri's red velvet cake. Though Lauren might be the more famous baker, Keri's talent was a known quantity. He couldn't go wrong with anything she'd made.

"Excellent choice," Keri said from the opposite side of the table as she extended a plastic knife and two forks.

He hadn't seen anyone else offered utensils.

"Which one did you choose?" Violet asked as she once again ushered her older sister where Violet evidently wanted her to go.

He lifted his prize. "Keri's red velvet."

"It looks delicious," Lauren said and smiled at Keri.

"I'm sure Adam can't eat the entire thing," Keri said. "Why don't you help him out?"

Adam suddenly felt as if he'd been sucked into one of Verona Charles's master matchmaking plans. And for once in his life he didn't mind.

"She's right," he said. "But if I take this home, I'll likely not get more than a single slice."

Lauren looked uncertain. "I need to tend to the girls."

"Two little babies don't need three people to take care of them," Violet said. "Papa Ed and I will be fine. We'll check out what else this lovely carnival has to offer."

Adam didn't miss the "you're going to pay for this later" look that Lauren shot her sister. But when she turned toward him, Lauren offered a smile.

"Looks like I get to enjoy some dessert. Been eyeing that cake all night."

Adam nodded toward the bleachers on the top level of the gym. "We can watch all the action from up there."

"Sounds good."

He led the way up the stairs, all the way to the top, where they could lean against the wall. Once they were seated, he handed her a fork then sliced two generous helpings. The moment Lauren took her first bite she closed her eyes and made an "mmm" of appreciation. Adam had to focus his attention on his own slice to keep from thinking about how that sound affected him.

"It's a good thing I'm opening a barbecue restaurant

instead of a bakery here," Lauren said. "The two things I've had that Keri made have been to die for."

"I'm sure your cake was delicious, too." As soon as the words left his mouth, he was fully aware of how annoyed he sounded.

"You don't like Tim, do you?"

He shrugged. "Friendly rivalry is all."

Lauren laughed in that way that said she didn't believe him. "I'm not sure friendly is how I'd describe it."

"Would you believe not openly hostile?"

"Yeah, barely."

"I hope that doesn't make you think worse of me."

"No, I understand. He's a bit full of himself. He tried to convince me that since he'd won dessert, we should go out to dinner first."

"I knew it." Adam shoved another bite of cake in his mouth.

"I wasn't going to go. He's not my type."

He looked over at her and decided not to hold in the question that surged to the front of his mind. "What is your type?"

"Honestly, I'm not sure. I thought I knew once, but that didn't turn out so well."

"Sorry. I didn't mean to bring up bad memories."

"No, it's okay. I can't let what happened rule the rest of my life." As soon as she said the words, she looked surprised. As if she hadn't meant to say them out loud or perhaps that she hadn't had the realization before that moment.

It was the closest thing to an opening as he was likely to get.

"If I was to ask you out, would you think I'm no better than Wainwright?"

"I know you're not the same as him, but I don't know if I'm ready for that."

"No pressure but we seem to get along well, and the truth is I really like you. Would it be easier if we started with a coffee?"

Lauren didn't answer. Instead, she cut off another bite of cake with her fork. As she ate it, she looked out over all the activity down on the gym floor. He followed her gaze and spotted her sister pushing the double stroller toward the ladies room.

"Poop happens," Lauren said.

"What?"

She pointed toward the bathroom. "Chances are either they've both gone doody in their diapers or one has and the other one will about the time Violet starts out of the bathroom."

"Oh. For a minute there I thought you were equating a date with me with poop."

"No, of course not."

He took encouragement from how strong her response was, how she seemed horrified he'd thought such a thing.

"Is that a yes, then?"

He noticed the death grip she had on her fork and wondered if she was imagining it was her ex's throat.

"Coffee and Danish at the bakery?" She sounded hesitant, as if she wasn't sure she was doing the right thing.

"Sounds great."

They settled on meeting the next morning before Lauren said she needed to get back to the hotel room and her family.

"I've been up since the crack of dawn, so I'm hitting the wall."

He covered the remainder of the cake and accompanied Lauren back down to the floor.

"Thanks for the cake," she said.

"You're welcome. Still curious what yours tastes like."

"Maybe you'll get the chance to find out sometime." The tentative smile that accompanied her words gave him hope that maybe their coffee date was just the beginning.

HAD SHE JUST agreed to go on a date with Adam, a man she truly didn't know all that well? By the smile he wore, she'd guess the answer was yes. She knew she should be more concerned, but oddly she wasn't. Like he said, no pressure. Just coffee and a Danish. It wasn't the same level of date seriousness as dinner, and since they were meeting at the bakery she could leave anytime she wanted.

Though would she really want to?

"See you tomorrow morning." Adam looked as if he wanted to hug her goodbye, maybe even plant a kiss on her cheek, but she wasn't ready for that—especially not in the midst of such a large crowd.

A crowd that included her sister, who'd taken one look at Adam and proceeded to push Lauren toward him. It was as if Violet had taken leave of her senses, developed sudden-onset amnesia regarding the past year and a half.

And yet Lauren had enjoyed sharing Adam's cake with him high above the carnival activity.

After Adam disappeared into the crowd that was beginning to thin a little, Lauren couldn't look away like she should have. Adam Hartley looked almost as good walking away as he did facing her.

"See anything interesting?" Violet's voice was full of the kind of teasing that had filled their teenage years.

Instead of answering her sister's question, Lauren turned toward Violet. "What was that?"

"What?" Violet did her best impersonation of innocence.

"You know what. You also know how I feel about getting involved with anyone else."

Then why did you agree to the breakfast date?

"Phil was the king of the asses, but he was only one guy. The best way to stick it to him is to be happy."

"I am happy."

"To a point. But you're young, beautiful and have a lot of love inside you to give."

"I give it every day to my daughters, you, Mom, Papa Ed."

"Not that kind of love. The kind that makes you feel whole and excited to wake up next to someone every morning."

"I had that and look where it got me."

"You didn't really have it, sis, because it didn't go both ways."

"And you think some near stranger with a red velvet cake is the one to change that?"

"Maybe. You two seemed to be having a nice time up there." Violet pointed toward the top level of the bleacher seating.

Lauren was tired of resisting a truth that she would never have expected to blossom at this point in her life—she really liked Adam, and not in a budding-friendship kind of way.

"Fine, you win."

"What did you win?" Papa Ed asked as he walked up with two tired babies in tow. The bright-eyed twins that had gloried in all the attention paid to them earlier now sported droopy eyelids.

Violet smiled, obviously satisfied with herself. "Lauren just admitted she likes Adam."

"He's a nice young man," Papa Ed said.

"Yeah, he is," Lauren said.

"You don't sound thrilled by that fact."

"It just complicates everything."

"Maybe you just think it does," he said. "No denying you were burned, and badly, but it makes my heart happy to think of you finally moving past it enough to even consider seeing someone else."

Lauren sighed. "It really doesn't make sense though. Even if it could be something, I'm not going to be here in Blue Falls forever. And I don't have it in me to do a long-distance relationship."

"Stop thinking about all the obstacles there could be in the future," Violet said. "Just enjoy the moment. Maybe it doesn't have to be anything other than a bit of fun, which you deserve."

Lauren looked down at her daughters. Harper was already asleep, and Bethany wasn't far behind.

"Don't even think about using these babies as an excuse why you can't go out. Plenty of single moms date."

"I'm aware."

"Now, how do you feel about asking him out?"

"No need."

"Lauren—"

"He already asked me to have coffee in the morning." For a moment, Violet didn't seem to comprehend.

But then her face lit up a moment before she squealed in obvious delight. The noise startled Bethany so much her eyes went wide.

"Sorry," Violet said as she soothed Bethany. "Go to sleep, sweetie."

That was all it took for Bethany's eyes to close. "How do you do that?" Lauren asked her baby-whisperer sister.

"They already know that I'm the cool aunt who will let them get away with all manner of mischief when they're older."

"If your sister doesn't disown you first."

"Aren't they just so precious?"

Lauren looked over to see Verona Charles eyeing the twins.

"Thank you. I think so."

Verona touched Lauren's shoulder in a gesture that said, "Of course you do, and rightly so."

"Verona Charles, I'd like you to meet my sister, Violet, and my grandfather—"

"Ed."

The sound of her grandfather's name spoken by Verona in such utter disbelief caused Lauren to look at the older woman. She appeared as if she might faint.

"Verona, are you okay?" Lauren reached toward the other woman in case she was having a stroke or a heart attack.

Instead of answering Lauren's question, Verona continued to stare at Papa Ed. And when Lauren shifted her gaze to her grandfather, he wore such an expression of sorrow that it was like seeing him the day of Nana Gloria's funeral all over again.

Before Lauren could ask what was going on, Verona took a sudden step back.

"Excuse me."

As she hurried away through the crowd, Lauren shifted her gaze to her grandfather again. "You know Verona?"

He didn't answer immediately, just continued to watch Verona until she disappeared out the door into the gym lobby. "A long time ago."

The look on his face said in no uncertain terms that there was way more to the story, but Lauren feared asking for specifics. Not while Papa Ed wore such a mournful look on his face.

Violet didn't have any such qualms, evidently. "Were you involved?"

Papa Ed finally pulled his gaze away from the door. "Not here. Not now."

Lauren realized he meant he didn't want to talk about it now. She had so many questions, but honestly, she wasn't sure she wanted to know the answers.

As he started walking toward the exit, Lauren and Violet stared after him and then at each other.

"I feel as if I just got dropped into another universe, where Papa Ed has secrets," Violet said.

That summed things up perfectly. Now that she thought about it, maybe an alternate reality also explained why she'd agreed to a date with Adam when Phil's betrayal still burned like a scorpion's sting.

Chapter Ten

"You looked like you were having fun last night," Angel said to Adam as he walked into the kitchen the next morning.

"I was." No sense in denying it, even though the cautious voice in his head still worried that he was making a mistake that would torpedo his business.

"So, when you going to ask her out?"

"Already did."

The surprise on his sister's face almost made him laugh.

"When? Where are you taking her? I need details."

"Now. The bakery."

Angel just stared at him as if he was lying. "You're taking a famous baker to a bakery for your first date?"

"Taking it slow."

Angel seemed to think about that for a moment. "You know, I think you're smarter than I give you credit for. Wise move."

"Well, now that I have my little sister's seal of approval..." he said with no small amount of sarcasm before heading toward the door.

As he drove toward town, a sudden wave of nervousness hit him. Normally, he wasn't prone to being nervous, especially not when going on a date. The fact that he was now told him that this—whatever it was with Lauren—was different. How different, he couldn't say.

When he arrived at the bakery, there was a line nearly out the door. He hadn't thought about all the pairs of eyes belonging to people he knew bearing witness to his date. People who would have questions and who would spread the sighting far and wide.

Oh, who was he kidding? The fact they'd sat in the gym away from everyone else while eating cake the night before likely was already setting the local grapevine on fire. It was just a fact of life in a small town.

Though the place was busy, most of the people were ordering to go. After stopping to talk to three different people in line, Adam finally made it to one of the small tables. He glanced at the time on his phone to find it was ten minutes past when he and Lauren were to meet. Had she heard enough local gossip to make her change her mind? She didn't seem like the type of person to stand him up without at least a text message. Just as he had that thought, she stepped through the front door. He considered it a good sign that she smiled as she approached the table, but as she drew closer he noticed how tired she looked. So much so that he was on the verge of asking if she'd had a bad night with the twins before thinking about how pointing out she looked tired probably wasn't the best way to start their date or get her to agree to a second one.

Instead, he stood to greet her. "Good morning."

"Good morning. Sorry I'm late."

Before he could respond, Karen Harrington, the head of the PTA at the school, came up to them.

"I just wanted to thank you for taking part in the

cakewalk last night," she said to Lauren. "We made more on that event than in the twenty-year history of the carnival."

"I'm glad to hear it." Lauren was no doubt sincere, but Adam heard the distraction in her voice.

After Karen headed toward the door, Adam asked, "Would you like to postpone this?" Part of him screamed inside his skull, asking him why he was giving her a chance to walk away and never say yes to a date with him again.

"No." Her answer wasn't particularly convincing, and she seemed to realize it. "Sorry. There's just something going on, family stuff."

"You won't hurt my feelings if you want to reschedule."

She shook her head. "No, it's definitely a 'maple-glazed doughnut' kind of morning."

"One maple-glazed doughnut coming right up. Coffee?"

"Yes, black and strong enough to walk by itself."

When Adam approached the front counter, Keri gave him a knowing grin. As he exchanged money for the order, she glanced to where Lauren sat at a small round table against the wall.

"You two are cute together."

He glanced toward his date, hoping Lauren thought so, too.

When he slipped not one but three maple-glazed doughnuts and a large coffee in front of her, Lauren looked up at him with the least amount of distraction in her expression since she'd arrived.

"You might be my new favorite person."

He smiled, liking the sound of that. "The power of sugar."

"Amen."

Adam sat opposite her and took a bite of his cruller. He watched as Lauren indulged in a huge bite of her first doughnut and dove into her coffee as if it was a life-saving device.

"WANT TO TALK about it?" Adam asked.

Lauren looked up from her coffee. "What?"

"Whatever is bothering you."

She placed her coffee cup back on the table slowly. "That obvious, huh?"

He held up his hand with the tips of his thumb and forefinger close to each other. "A little."

"I'm not entirely sure what it is."

He gave her a curious expression, so she leaned her forearms on the table. "What do you know about Verona Charles?"

Judging by the look on his face, her question wasn't even in the ballpark of what he might have expected.

"She's retired from the tourist bureau. Her niece owns the garden center outside town. And she's the self-appointed matchmaker of Blue Falls." All of which he'd told her before.

"Single?"

"Uh, yeah. Don't think she ever married. Honestly, I've never even seen her out with anyone. Why?"

"We ran into her at the carnival right after you left, and it was obvious she and Papa Ed knew each other. They both looked like they'd received a shock from those paddles they use to restart people's hearts."

"Has he ever mentioned her before?"

"No. In fact, he's always said that he's been gone from Blue Falls so long that he doesn't know anyone from here anymore."

"Did you ask him about it?"

"Yes, not that it did us any good. I've never known him to be so silent on a subject."

"And that has you worried."

"Not really." She sounded as if she wasn't sure of her answer. "Maybe some. It's just so atypical I don't know what to think."

"Gossip being what it is, I'm sure someone knows something if you ask around."

"Don't think I haven't thought about it, but I owe it to Papa Ed to wait until he's ready to share." No matter how hard that might prove to be.

She watched as Adam took a drink of his coffee, as he swallowed. Though he wasn't dressed up, there was no mistaking how handsome he was. Or the fact he was perceptive enough to know something was bothering her. Had Phil ever been that attentive to her moods and feelings? Why had she overlooked the fact he most likely hadn't? Love really did make you blind.

And that made love dangerous.

But there was no reason to worry about that in the current situation. Right? She worried when the answer didn't easily present itself.

"I'm sorry to go on about personal stuff," she said.

"I thought that's what dates were for—to share at least some personal details with each other. Granted, I'm a little rusty."

"At what?" Surely he didn't mean dating, but he hadn't mentioned anything else.

"Honestly, it's been a while since I've been out with anyone."

"I find that hard to believe."

"So either you think I'm a liar or so irresistible that I have dates lined up for miles."

Lauren opened her mouth to respond before she realized she didn't know how. After a moment, Adam laughed.

"It's neither," he said.

"So why haven't you been on a date recently?" Better to talk about his reasons than hers.

He shrugged. "Busy, I guess. Ranches don't run themselves, and I've been putting a lot of time into trying to build the branded-beef business."

She parsed his words, trying to determine if he was aiming to get her to commit to working with him. When she didn't find any pressure directed at her, she was thankful. Because if she decided to go out with him again, there would be no business deal between them. Never again was she mixing business with pleasure.

And pleasure was what she was increasingly thinking of when she was around Adam. Even when she wasn't and simply thought about him. She wondered if his interest in her would disappear if she told him the loss of a contract was the price of going out with her.

Lauren yanked back on her thoughts. She was getting ahead of herself. There was no guarantee that they would see each other again after they shared this one breakfast. Did she even want to?

Yes.

The answer came to her with a speed and certainty that scared her. She really liked him, enjoyed spending time with him. She just hoped she wasn't making another mistake. How was she supposed to know for sure?

"I used to think that all work and no play wasn't the way to live one's life, but I'm not sure anymore."

"Because of your ex-fiancé?"

"Yeah. It's hard to trust after someone betrays you."

"True." He sounded as if he was speaking from experience, and the thought that someone had betrayed him as well caused her anger to heat a few degrees.

"Did someone hurt you?"

He shook his head. "No, but I've seen the effect on some of my brothers and sisters."

Her thoughts went immediately to Angel and the fact that Julia's father didn't seem to be in the picture. But even though she felt herself getting gradually closer to Adam, it wasn't close enough to ask about his sister's situation. Angel's story wasn't her brother's to tell.

"You ever think there are way too many crappy people in the world?"

"More times than I can count. And if you don't mind me saying so, your ex is near the top of that list. He's an idiot for hurting you and his daughters."

The sincerity in Adam's words touched her so deeply that tears sprang to her eyes. "Thank you."

Adam reached across the table and took her hand in his. He gave it a reassuring squeeze. Even though it was gentle, she felt a silent offer of his strength if she needed it. When she met his gaze, she saw the same and it caused a warm, tingly feeling to travel across her skin before sinking down deep into her heart.

The fear she had of trusting a man again made a valiant effort to assert itself, but her growing affection for Adam beat it back.

"You don't have to talk about it, but if you ever want to, I'll listen. I don't know if I can offer anything of value in response, but sometimes it just helps to get it out."

"More experience with your brothers and sisters?"

He nodded. "Really, I think it applies to everyone, even someone who hasn't had it as bad as other people."

Was he saying that compared to his siblings, he'd had an easy past? If so, she couldn't imagine what they'd been through because losing one's entire family at a young age wasn't exactly a "rainbows and puppies" type of childhood.

This time she squeezed his hand. "Don't give your own pain less weight just because others might have more or different traumas to deal with."

His eyes reflected surprise, and then they softened in a way that made her want very much to be taken into his arms. When Adam moved his hand so that he laced his fingers with hers, she wondered if he could read her thoughts.

"I know it's probably hard to trust someone after what your ex did to you, but I like you, Lauren. A lot. And I'd like to take you out on a proper date if you'll let me."

Her heart screamed *Yes!* But her mind, which tended to search constantly for threats to her and her family, for flaws in her own judgment, told her to proceed with caution.

"That sounds nice, but I don't know. I already leave the girls with my sister and grandfather too often."

"We can take the twins with us."

She stared at him, suddenly wondering if he had

some sort of angle. "You want to take two teething babies on a date with us?"

"Sure, why not?"

"Um, because they're teething babies, and they tend to cry." Which didn't seem like the most romantic image in her mind.

Though his willingness to include Harper and Bethany certainly was.

"We could go to the Christmas parade and then the ice-sculpture exhibit in Austin. Angel took Julia a couple of times and she loved it."

He was actually serious. She searched for any indication his offer was a joke or some plot to gain something for himself, particularly anything that would benefit his bottom line. But either she was still as blind as she'd been with Phil, or it wasn't there. She didn't think she could adequately express how much she hoped it was the latter.

"Okay." She'd go in with her eyes open this time, but there was no denying that she wanted to spend more time with Adam.

The wide smile that spread across his face filled her heart with something it hadn't felt in a while—hope.

LAUREN FINISHED BUNDLING Bethany in her little red outfit that sported dancing reindeer across the front and then gave her a gentle tap on the end of her nose, making her daughter laugh. Spurred by her sister's giggles, Harper—wearing a similar green outfit with dancing candy canes—joined in.

"They sound as if they're ready for a night on the town," Violet said.

"If only their mom could be as carefree." Lauren

placed a hand against her unsettled stomach. "Am I making a mistake dating so soon?"

"It's not that soon."

"Still."

"Has Adam said or done anything suspicious? Remotely Phil-like?"

"No."

"Then why would it be a mistake?"

"Lots of reasons, not the least of which is the fact that my plate is already full. Beyond full."

"You, of all people, should know there's always room for dessert."

Lauren's cheeks heated at the thought of tasting Adam like a decadent dessert.

"I'd bet every dime I have in the bank that you're having naughty thoughts right now," Violet said with mischief in her voice.

"Oh, shut up." Lauren looked around the hotel room as if she might miraculously find an ally. Not even Papa Ed was around. The day after the winter carnival and the awkward interaction with Verona, he'd borrowed Violet's car, claiming he had to go home to take care of some things.

Neither she nor Violet had bought the explanation for his hasty departure, but the look on his face had been enough to keep them from probing for a more believable reason.

And even though she'd spotted Verona across the street when she'd left the Mehlerhaus Bakery with Adam after their breakfast date, the town's self-professed matchmaker had made herself scarce. Lauren might have chalked it up to the other woman being busy, but Adam had said Verona was never too busy to miss an opportunity to push two people toward each other, especially if they were already pointed in the right direction.

"Have you heard from Papa Ed?"

Violet's expression changed to one of concern. "No. But don't think about that now. Tonight you are to have fun with your babies and that sexy rancher."

"And what exactly are you going to do with your evening?"

"My job. And if I happen to need something to drink and that need takes me to the music hall, where I might find a sexy cowboy of my own, well, who am I to argue with Fate?"

Lauren snorted at her sister then remembered what had happened to her when she'd gone to the music hall alone. She still hadn't told anyone about that incident, but she had to break that silence now.

"Be careful if you go out," she said, then told Violet about her run-in with the two drunk men and how Adam had come to her aid.

"I suddenly like Adam a whole lot more," Violet said when Lauren finished telling her about that night.

"Don't tell Mom or Papa Ed about what happened. I don't want them to worry." Or to read too much into her relationship with Adam before she even knew how serious it might become. She still wasn't sure agreeing to go out with him was wise, but she was finding it more and more difficult to deny what she wanted.

Lauren was so lost in her thoughts that she jumped when someone knocked on the door. Before she could answer it, Violet gripped Lauren's shoulders and all hint of teasing was gone from her expression.

"Try to have a good time. You deserve to be happy,

and from what I've seen, spending time with Adam makes you happy."

"I'm just so scared to hope for too much."

"Maybe Adam is your reward for having to go through what you did with Phil."

Lauren liked that idea, and when she opened the door and saw Adam standing there in all his tall, dark-haired, heartwarming-smile glory, she admitted to herself that it would be really easy to fall for him despite how badly she'd been burned before. She hoped with all her heart that Violet was right and Adam Hartley was the universe's way of balancing the scales of Lauren's life, giving her someone who was as good as Phil was bad.

Chapter Eleven

Adam's heart sped up at the sight of Lauren when she opened the door to her hotel room. It wasn't as if she was dressed appropriately for four-star dining. It had nothing to do with her casual attire, fit for a night out with her babies as companions, but rather there was something new in her eyes. She looked glad to see him instead of afraid he was one step away from betraying her trust. He'd never wanted to prove himself to someone so much in his life, not even his parents when they'd adopted him.

"You look beautiful." He didn't know he'd been about to say those words until they tumbled out of his mouth, but he'd never uttered anything truer.

Lauren's eyes widened a fraction, and she looked flustered by his compliment.

"Uh, thanks." She looked down at the red sweater she wore as if it had magically transformed into a designer gown, like the kind actresses wore to big award shows.

"You ready to head out?"

She looked up at him and the flustered expression had been replaced by a smile that warmed him all over.

"Your chaperones are ready to blow this joint," Violet said as she rolled the double stroller toward the door.

She crouched next to the babies. "I'm trusting you to watch those two and make sure they have tons of fun."

Adam laughed at the sight of Lauren rolling her eyes at her younger sister.

It took a few minutes to get the kids loaded into the car seats they put in the back seat of his mom's SUV. As Lauren secured Bethany, he did the same for Harper and checked to make sure he'd done it right three times. He wasn't going to put Lauren or her twins in any unnecessary danger.

When he and Lauren belted themselves into their seats, Lauren reached across and placed her hand atop his.

"Thank you," she said.

"For what?"

"Taking such care with Harper, for being willing to bring them with us."

"Are you kidding? I get three lovely dates instead of one."

She smiled at that, which caused that warm, tingly feeling all over his body again. The fact he'd never felt anything like it before told him he was falling for her. He didn't know if or how things would work out for them, considering it wasn't a path without obstacles, but he'd take each day and each interaction one at a time in the hope that she would be willing to walk that path with him.

"Plus," he said as he started the engine, "having kids with me gives me a legitimate reason to go down a slide made of ice."

"Oh, well, as long as you don't have an ulterior motive," Lauren said with a laugh.

By the time they reached Austin, the parade route

was already filling up with spectators. Adam lucked into a decent parking space and helped Lauren bundle up the girls against the chill.

"It'll probably be easier in this crowd to just carry them," he said as Lauren moved to the back of the SUV to retrieve the stroller.

"They might be small but they get heavy pretty quickly."

"You know what's heavier? Bales of hay." He gave an exaggerated flex of his biceps.

Lauren laughed at his antics. "Remember I warned you."

Making Lauren laugh gave him the best feeling, one he wouldn't mind being a constant companion.

As they searched for a good spot to watch the parade, he carried Harper while Lauren held Bethany. He stepped onto a section of curb vacated by a mom and a wailing youngster who'd obviously gotten in trouble and thus given up his right to watch the parade. Just as Adam ushered Lauren in beside him, a siren announced the beginning of the parade.

"Good timing," Lauren said.

As the siren drew closer, Harper jumped in his arms and let out a cry.

"Now, now," he said as he distracted her by making funny faces.

When Bethany expressed her displeasure at the loud noise, Lauren covered the child's ears.

"Maybe this wasn't such a good idea," Lauren said.

Adam couldn't let her doubts cause her to back out now. Because despite the fact that the noise was indeed bothering the twins, he had no doubt that Lauren's fear of getting involved with someone again was

at the root of her sudden hint that they leave. He pro-
tected Harper's little ears with his chest and free hand
as the police cruiser come closer.

"The siren will be past in a minute." Adam wasn't
giving up on this date—or Lauren—that easily. He had
the feeling she needed this as much as he wanted it.

Lauren and the girls seemed to relax as the police
car gave way to decorated floats, troops of uniformed
scouts and bands playing Christmas carols. When he
glanced over and saw Lauren smiling as she pointed
out to Bethany a person dressed as that snowman from
Frozen, his heart felt abnormally full. In this moment,
he felt as if they were a family and he liked the feeling
more than he'd ever expected.

He suspected Lauren's arms were getting tired when
she shifted Bethany from one to the other.

"Give her here," he said.

"You already have your arms full."

"This little bit?" He jostled Harper playfully, making
her laugh. What was it about baby laughter that made
all seem right with the world? He remembered having
the same feeling when Julia was a baby, and how his
niece's peals of laughter had helped Angel get through
those early days of single motherhood with her heart
and sanity intact. Did Lauren feel the same?

He scooped Bethany out of Lauren's arms, and the
twins seemed to be delighted to be in close proximity
again. Lauren stepped closer to him, her arm brush-
ing his, to allow a couple to pass from the street to the
sidewalk behind him. When Lauren didn't move away
after the man and woman had made their way by, he
tried not to grin like the luckiest man in the world.
It was early in his and Lauren's relationship, with no

guarantee it would progress, but in this moment he felt as if this was one of those big turning points in his life he'd look back on with fondness when he was an old man surrounded by grandchildren. He couldn't help but wonder if Bethany and Harper would be the ones to give him those grandchildren.

With his heart speeding up, he looked over at Lauren and envisioned having even more children with her, of making and growing a family together that would fill in some more empty spaces on the Rocking Horse Ranch.

And in their hearts.

LAUREN HELD ON tightly to Bethany as they sped down a slide made of ice descending from an ice castle. Bethany's infectious giggles filled Lauren's heart nearly to bursting. When it came right down to it, the thing she wanted most in the world was to make sure her daughters had a safe and happy childhood. Tonight, Adam was helping her fulfill that wish. Not once had she seen any indication that bringing the twins along on their date annoyed Adam in any way. He really did appear to be having fun with them. When she started to think about how sad it was that their own father wasn't the one giving them these experiences and making them laugh, she forcefully shoved away thoughts of Phil. She didn't want him intruding on this outing.

At the bottom of the slide, she stood and held Bethany close as they watched Adam approach the top of the slide with Harper. The fact she wasn't nervous about Harper's safety told her that Adam had earned her trust—a realization that stunned her.

But it was more than trust she was feeling for Adam, wasn't it?

She doubted all her concerns about trusting too easily had disappeared for good, but tonight they seemed to have at least taken a vacation. And the truth was it felt good to not be so guarded. It felt as if she'd been walking around with all of her muscles tensed, as if prepared for an attack, and now they'd finally relaxed, allowing her to rest and enjoy living in the moment without dwelling on the past or worrying about the future.

"He's really good with your babies."

Lauren looked over to a worker dressed as one of Santa's elves. The woman seemed to have assumed that they were a couple, that Adam was the twins' father.

She found she didn't want to correct the woman's erroneous assumption. For one night she wanted to just pretend she was part of a happy, whole family. And that she was with a man who was honest, kind and loved her daughters—and maybe could love her as well.

Realizing the elf woman was staring at her, Lauren smiled. "Yes, he is," she said, before the other woman smiled and walked away.

With a "whee!" that would be more at home coming from a child, Adam pushed off from the top of the slide with Harper. The wave of laughter coming from Harper brought tears of happiness to Lauren's eyes. They must have still been there when Adam stood and made eye contact with her.

The joy faded from his face. "Are you okay?"

She nodded.

"But you look like you're about to cry." The concern in his voice just added to the rising well of feeling in her chest.

"Just really happy. Thank you for all this."

Adam took a slow step toward her. Were it not for the fact they each held a baby, she thought he might kiss her. And she might let him.

More than might.

When he lifted his hand to cup her jaw and run a thumb across her cheek that was warm despite their frozen surroundings, she wondered if he was going to kiss her anyway.

"You're welcome." It was a simple response, one she might expect, but the way he was looking at her said so much more.

If she didn't look away, the heat building in her body was going to melt the ice palace and turn this wintry attraction into an indoor whitewater river instead.

After what seemed like hours of staring into Adam's eyes, Lauren became aware that they were standing in the way of other people waiting to descend the slide. Adam's hand dropped away from her face but resettled at the small of her back as they moved on to the next exhibit—a small carousel made of colored ice.

"It's amazing…everything they have in here," Lauren said.

"Yeah, it is."

Something about the tone of Adam's voice drew her attention back to him. Instead of admiring the craftsmanship of the ice carvers, he instead was looking at her as if she was some sort of masterpiece.

Had Phil ever looked at her that way? She knew the answer before the question fully formed. Looking back now, she could see how blind she'd been. Granted, Phil had been good at acting his role as devoted and loving fiancé, but in the wake of his betrayal it was as if a veil hiding his true intent had been lifted from her eyes—one that hid the fact Phil had only cared for himself.

Try as she might, she detected no veil with Adam. She sent up a silent prayer that she wasn't wrong.

He'd just finished taking some photos of her holding the girls in a scene of the North Pole made of ice when another worker dressed as an elf walked up to Adam.

"I can take a picture of all of you together if you'd like."

When Lauren saw Adam about to decline, she said, "Thanks. That's nice of you."

Adam's quick look of surprise gave way to a smile as he handed over her phone and moved to join her and the girls. He didn't say anything as he took Harper from her then wrapped his arm around Lauren's shoulders and pulled her close as if he'd done it a thousand times before. A lump formed in her throat at the thought that she wanted this picture-perfect family scene to be real.

"Give me some big smiles," the elf lady said.

Complying wasn't difficult. In fact, Lauren found it easier to smile in that moment than she had in a long time.

By the time they left the ice palace and grabbed a quick dinner at a gourmet burger place, the girls were tired and getting fussy.

"Sorry," Lauren said as Bethany let out a wail that turned the head of everyone on the sidewalk for a solid block as Lauren and Adam walked back toward his mom's SUV.

"No need to apologize. It's not the first time I've been around a cranky baby. Nothing's going to beat when Julia had colic. I thought her cries might bring down the roof of the house on top of all of us."

Lauren tried to imagine Phil being so understanding and couldn't picture it. Of course, he'd purposely raised doubts about whether the twins were his, even though she'd given him no reason to question her faithfulness.

Neither she nor Adam spoke again until they were on the road heading out the western edge of Austin and the girls had fallen asleep in their car seats. Lauren gazed out her window at the occasional brightly colored Christmas tree in someone's window, or a yard filled with inflatable representations of holiday cheer. She relished the peace and quiet. And thought about how this moment never would have happened with Phil. She couldn't imagine him acting like a child as he headed down a slide made of ice. If she was being honest with herself, she couldn't even picture him holding his daughters. Especially not with undisguised affection the way Adam did.

"You're thinking about him again, aren't you?"

She turned her head to look at Adam. He glanced at her and there was still enough light from their surroundings that she saw the unsure expression on his face. Somehow she knew it wasn't his question he was unsure of, but whether he should have asked it. Oddly, a part of her was glad he had. It showed he paid attention, was concerned about her.

"How could you tell?"

"You get a different look in your eyes—as if your mind has traveled somewhere else—and you go quiet."

"I'm sorry."

Adam took her hand and squeezed. "You keep apologizing for things you don't need to."

"It's just that crying babies and my wandering thoughts probably aren't your idea of a good date."

"Have you heard me complain?"

"Well, no, but—"

"No *buts*. If I minded you bringing the girls, I wouldn't have suggested it. I do, however, wish you could enjoy yourself without thoughts of your ex invading."

"I'm—" She caught herself mid-apology. "It's hard not to see the world through a different lens now."

"I understand."

Maybe he thought he did, but how could he when he didn't know the whole story?

"Did I do something that reminded you of him?"

"No," she said, but then realized that was actually a lie. "I mean, yes, but in a good way."

He glanced at her briefly before returning his attention to the highway. "That's going to require more explanation."

"I was just thinking I couldn't imagine Phil actually having fun at the ice palace."

"Not even for his daughters?"

"Considering he has barely acknowledged their existence and even tried to claim in court they weren't his, no."

"He thought you'd been with someone else?"

The way Adam sounded as he posed the question—as if he couldn't fathom her cheating in a million years—caused a strange fluttering sensation in her chest.

"More like he was looking for any way he could to punish me."

"For what?"

"For ruining his grand plan to use me as his gravy train."

The look of confusion visible even by viewing only Adam's profile told her he hadn't dug too deeply into the details of the trial.

For the first time, she found herself wanting to share what had happened. When she'd had to reveal everything before, it hadn't been of her choosing. She'd been in a courtroom, forced to stick only to facts with little explanation allowed. Even though she'd won the case, thinking about the ordeal still made her feel raw and exposed.

"You don't have to explain," he said.

But there was something about riding along in the dark and not actually facing him that made it easier for the words to start tumbling out.

"Phil and I were together almost two years. I thought I knew him or I would have never agreed to marry him. But it turned out I didn't really know him at all."

When Adam didn't ask any questions, and instead gave her the freedom to reveal as much or little as she wanted, Lauren took a deep breath and dove into the telling of the most exhausting time of her life.

"I've been trying not to feel like a fool ever since I found out Phil wasn't the person I thought. Some days are harder than others." Like when the fear she'd make the same mistake again reared its head. "I found out he was making promises of business deals for my company without my knowledge. He was signing contracts and taking money when he had no legal right to do so. I didn't want to believe it and couldn't bring myself to confront him—at least not until I was certain. Violet convinced me to hire a private investigator. I still get sick at my stomach thinking about it. I was so afraid of what he'd find or if there was no evidence of wrongdoing Phil would feel betrayed and leave."

"But he did find something," Adam said after a few seconds, making her realize she'd lapsed into silence.

"Yeah. The PI posed as someone wanting to do business with Brazos Baker, and Phil went through with signing a fake contract, claiming he spoke for the company. One, he wasn't an employee. And we weren't married, so even that tie wasn't there. He had his own job as a salesman for a company that sells commercial kitchen supplies. That's how we met—at a trade show for chefs."

She'd once thought if she could go back in time, she'd skip that trade show and thus avoid Phil being a part of her life completely. But then she wouldn't have Bethany and Harper, and despite how frazzled and tired she often felt, she couldn't imagine her life without them now.

"I confronted Phil about it and he tried to wave it off as a misunderstanding. That was until I slapped the evidence from the PI down in front of him. Then he got angry, said I was just trying to find an excuse to get out of the marriage and giving him what he was owed. He was talking nonsense and continued to do so with his attorney. I think the guy actually believed Phil's lies."

"Did he claim he acted on your authority?"

"Yes, and when he couldn't provide proof of that, he claimed that I'd promised him half the company as a wedding present. I'd done no such thing, and he actually shot himself in the foot with that claim because an attorney came forward with evidence that Phil had him draw up a prenuptial agreement." Lauren swallowed the bile rising in her throat. "He intended to get me to agree to it and rob me of half of what I'd worked so hard to build."

Adam reached over and took her hand in his. She latched on to his support before getting to the worst part of the story.

"I sense there's more," he said.

"When I found out I was pregnant, I still felt I should tell him he was going to be a father. A part of me thought it would make him back down, that it would change his entire outlook on things. Instead, he had his attorney blindside me in court, claiming the girls weren't his. He knew they were, and a DNA test proved it. He just wanted to embarrass me, make my viewers question the entire wholesome, family-centered tone of my business. If he couldn't have what he wanted, he didn't intend for me to have it, either."

"Please tell me he's rotting in a prison cell for fraud."

How many times had Lauren fantasized about that very thing?

"No."

"I thought he lost the case."

"He did. It was my choice. It took some convincing of the people he'd conned, the judge, even my own attorney, but everyone finally agreed that it was better he remain free so he could make reparations and do a boatload of community service."

"Why did you let him off so easy?"

"Because his going to jail would have just made bigger headlines, and I wanted all the negative attention to go away so I could move on and do damage control." She paused, took a shaky breath. "And because I didn't want the girls to grow up with the stigma of having a father in prison."

Adam was quiet for a long moment, one during which Lauren wondered if he now thought she was the fool she feared.

"You're a good mother. A great one."

"Thank you," she said, her throat full of rising emotion she couldn't name.

Or was too scared to.

Chapter Twelve

Adam didn't typically have violent tendencies, even less so than his normally pretty chill brothers. But the more Lauren told him about what Phil had done, the more he wanted to punch the guy into another galaxy. The thought of the jerk walking around free—even if he had lost his job and now had to do court-ordered community service, no doubt working as part of a sanitation crew—just didn't seem right. The fact that Lauren had set aside her own hurt, and probably desire for revenge, in order to protect her daughters said a lot about the kind of person she was—the kind he liked more with each passing minute.

When he pulled in to the parking lot of the Wildflower Inn, he wished the drive back had been longer. He didn't want the night to end, but with two babies to get to bed, there was no chance of it extending further than the next few minutes.

He expected Lauren to get out of the SUV as soon as he parked. Instead, she sat staring out the windshield toward the dark surface of Blue Falls Lake.

"Other than family and attorneys, you're the only person I've told any of that," she said.

Though he wished she hadn't been put through such

hell, he felt honored she trusted him enough to share the details with him—especially when he knew trust was a huge obstacle for her.

"For what it's worth, you're one of the strongest women I've ever met. Not a lot of people could have gone through what you did without coming out the other side bitter and angry."

"Oh, trust me there's been plenty of that."

"But it doesn't rule you. It's not what people see when they meet you."

She looked at him and he'd swear he'd never seen anyone so beautiful; she didn't even have to be in full light for it to show.

"What do they see?"

He stared at her, wanting to pull her into his arms and kiss her until they both were forced to surface for oxygen.

"*They* or me?"

Lauren didn't respond at first, instead licking her lips. "You."

He cupped her jaw, loving the feel of her soft skin against his rougher palm. "A woman who is strong, caring, hardworking and so beautiful I sometimes forget how to form words."

She placed her palm against the hand he held to her cheek and swallowed visibly. "Thank you. I haven't heard anything like that in a long time—and then only from someone who probably didn't mean it."

"Which in itself is a crime."

Lauren lowered her gaze, appearing as if she had no idea how to respond.

Adam started to lean toward her, but one of the girls

made a sound in the back, dispersing any romantic thoughts Lauren might have been entertaining.

"I better get them inside. I don't want them getting too cold."

The interior of the SUV might have been cooling now that the engine and thus the heater weren't running, but Adam hadn't noticed. His blood had heated at Lauren's nearness, at the fact she hadn't pulled away, even more so when he'd thought they might finally share a kiss.

The speed with which she opened her door and slipped out caused him to wonder if it had less to do with getting the babies inside and a lot more with the fact he'd spooked her. What he'd said about her being strong was true, but he had to wonder if Phil's actions had done more damage than Lauren realized.

With a sigh, he got out as well, aiming to retrieve Harper from her seat behind his. When they reached Lauren's room with the babies still half-asleep a few minutes later, he handed Harper off to Violet. He noticed Lauren's sister glancing between them, no doubt curious how the date went. He'd likely encounter similar curiosity when he arrived home. The thought made him halfway want to get a room here at the inn tonight.

Of course, that thought made him think of how he might use that room.

When Lauren turned to say good-night, he wondered if she could see his thoughts. Especially when he considered she wore a smile that was shyer than he knew her to be.

"Thanks for tonight," she said. "I had a nice time. And though they can't say it yet, the girls did, too."

He nodded. "Me, too." The moment grew awkward. "Well, good night."

"Good night."

During his walk back to the parking lot, an odd emptiness accompanied him. A feeling of being incomplete. He walked a few feet past his mom's SUV to the grassy crest of the hill that led down to the lakeside park. He shivered against a sudden brisk wind off the lake that eliminated what little of his earlier warmth still lingered.

"Adam?"

At first he thought he'd imagined Lauren's voice, but then he heard footsteps behind him. He turned to find her standing a short distance away.

"Is everything okay?" he asked.

She appeared to be about to say something, but in the next moment she erased the few feet between them, placed her hands on his shoulders and lifted onto her toes. As her lips touched his, Adam wrapped his arms around her and pulled her even closer.

And the incomplete feeling went completely away.

LAUREN LET GO of the last bit of resistance holding her back and fell completely into the kiss. When Adam's arms came around her, pulling her closer, she didn't think she'd ever loved the feel of anything more.

Though the air around them was cold enough she'd seen her breath on the walk out here, she was fairly certain flames were licking at her body. Were it not for her sister and daughters inside, she would lead Adam back to the room and see where things went. It'd been so long since she'd been held by a man, since she'd felt any passion.

Truth was she'd never felt a hunger like what was gnawing at her now. She wanted Adam, all of him, more than she could adequately describe. That should scare her, would have only minutes ago, but in this moment it didn't. Because crossing this line had been her move. He'd given her that. And now he was showing her just how much he had been holding back. Because there was no way the hunger she felt from him had just been born when she captured his lips with hers.

She had no idea how much time had elapsed when their lips finally left each other. Were it not for Adam's hands against her back, Lauren would have been pretty certain she would have stumbled and perhaps toppled right over. The feeling in her head was similar to the dizzy feeling she got when on a boat.

"I'm sorry," Adam said, sounding breathless. "Too much?"

Not enough. Not nearly enough.

"Don't apologize. I seem to remember I started that."

A slow, sexy grin transformed Adam from apologist to a man she was having an extraordinarily hard time not shoving into the back seat of his mom's SUV and steaming up the windows so much that someone was bound to call the cops.

That mental image caused her to laugh, which wiped the grin from Adam's face.

"My turn to apologize," she said as she motioned toward her head. "Inappropriate thoughts."

The grin raced back to his mouth. "That right?"

"And no, I'm not sharing them."

Adam tugged her closer, and there was no mistaking just what kind of effect their hot make-out session had on him. Honestly, she was surprised there wasn't visible steam coming off her own body.

Lauren thought about how she'd run out on Violet without an explanation, not that she didn't think her sister had already come up with something juicy. "I should get back inside."

"Can't say I like that idea."

She smiled up at Adam and hoped with all her might that he was the good guy he seemed. "I should be scared out of my mind right now, but I'm not."

Adam ran the tips of his fingers softly along the edge of her face. "Does that mean you'll go out with me again?"

"Yes. And maybe I can arrange a babysitter next time." She hated to keep depending on her family to look after the girls so much, but if she didn't get some alone time with Adam she was afraid she might combust. Maybe she could hire a babysitter and give them all a free night.

"As cute as the girls are, I like the sound of that."

Though she didn't want to, she made herself take a step backward and then another. "I'll let you know, okay?"

Another step and the only part of them that was still touching was their hands, but then Adam pulled her quickly back into his arms and kissed her again—a deep, thorough kiss that left her wondering if she had enough energy left to walk back to the room.

"I better let you go before I act on some of my own inappropriate thoughts," he said, but then gave her another mind-spinning kiss before breaking all contact and stepping toward the SUV. "I'll wait until you get inside."

Inside the SUV? Yes, please.

But no, he meant the inn. Somehow she remembered how walking worked, so she turned and headed for the light of the lobby. She didn't allow herself to look back at Adam or she might walk right back to him. Possibly run. Her entire body was shaking as she entered the light and warmth of the lobby. A quick glance toward the check-in desk revealed that the young woman there appeared to be hiding a smile. Had she seen Lauren and Adam getting hot and heavy in the parking lot?

Good grief, she had to be careful. Everyone had a cell phone, and the last thing she needed was a video of her and Adam all over each other in a dark parking lot hitting the internet. It would shoot all her work to put the coverage of the trial and questions about her morality firmly behind her and out of the minds of her viewers.

She walked on legs that felt like overcooked noodles down the hallway toward her room. When she reached it, she didn't immediately enter. Instead, she leaned against the wall and tried to get her breathing under control. To slow her heart rate. To formulate some sort of response to the questions she knew waited for her on the other side of the door.

She caught movement out of the corner of her eye, and her heart jumped into her throat. When she turned toward the end of the corridor, she fully expected to see Phil staring at her. She'd swear she saw him. Anger propelled her down the hallway. When she reached him, she was going to fire at him with both barrels with everything she'd imagined saying to him that she hadn't been able to in that courtroom. Punish him for intruding on this moment when she was basking in the glow of having kissed Adam.

But when she reached the end of the hallway and looked in both directions, there was no one in sight. And there was nowhere he could have hidden that quickly. She'd imagined him. Was this the universe's way of warning her she was making a mistake again?

No, Adam was a good guy. He'd proven that over and over, hadn't he?

With a sigh, she turned and walked back to her room. She took a deep breath and pulled the key card out of her pocket. But before she could slip it into the slot, the exit door at the end of the hall opened and she jerked toward the sound. But it still wasn't Phil. Instead, Papa Ed stepped inside. Had he arrived back while she was gone to Austin? If so, why had he just been outside? Surely he hadn't driven back this late.

What worried her more than his driving several hours alone after dark was how he appeared to be carrying a heavy but invisible burden on his shoulders.

"Papa Ed?"

He looked up as he neared her, seeming startled to find her out in the corridor.

"Did you just get back?"

He gave a quick nod, looking as if he wanted nothing more than to slip inside his room and fall asleep. But he halted midway to reaching for his door and turned toward her.

"Is Violet awake?"

"Yeah."

"I'd like to talk to you both."

Something cold and foreboding settled in the pit of her stomach. "Is Mom okay?"

"She's fine, honey. And before you ask, I'm okay, too. I just have something I need to talk to you about."

Despite what he said, it had to be something serious if he wasn't willing to wait until morning. Before she allowed her mind to jump to all kinds of horrible conclusions, she slipped her key in the door and eased inside so as not to wake up the girls.

Violet jumped up from where she sat at the small desk working on the computer with an excited look on her face, all those questions Lauren had imagined shining in her sister's eyes—until she saw Papa Ed behind her.

"What's wrong?"

Lauren gave a little shake of her head as she checked the girls and saw they were fast asleep. She also noticed that Violet had gotten a miniature lighted Christmas tree from somewhere and placed it on top of the small fridge. It'd be enough to make Lauren smile if she wasn't so concerned about Papa Ed. She had the awful feeling that after the most wonderful night she'd had in ages, a bomb was about to be dropped on her life yet again.

Suddenly exhausted, she sank onto the side of her bed. She watched as Papa Ed walked over to where his great-granddaughters were sleeping. He smiled as he looked down at them.

"They really are the most beautiful little girls," he said.

"Papa Ed, tell us what's going on. You're freaking me out," Violet said.

Lauren couldn't have more perfectly voiced her feelings as her grandfather sat on Violet's bed. She noticed him fidgeting with the fabric of his pants, as if nervous. It wasn't a state in which she'd very often seen him. Just as she was about to ask him again what was wrong, he took a deep breath and began to speak.

"I know you have been curious about that incident with Verona Charles at the carnival," he said. "The simple answer is that we used to know each other a long time ago."

"And the 'not simple' answer?" Lauren prompted. "Was she an old girlfriend?" It was hard to imagine him with anyone other than Nana Gloria, but she knew they'd had lives before they'd gotten married.

He nodded. "We were pretty serious." He paused, as if the weight of the past was crushing him. "I loved her."

Lauren glanced at Violet, whose eyes had widened at that revelation, before she returned her attention to Papa Ed. "What happened?"

"I had dated your grandmother before Verona and I got together, and…well, your mother was the result."

It was as if Lauren's brain encountered a thick bank of fog, preventing it from processing her grandfather's meaning. But then Violet gasped, jerking Lauren out of the fog as if she'd been lassoed and yanked out by a speeding horse.

"Explain." It was the only word she could get past her lips, though she was beginning to form a picture in her mind.

"It was a different time then, so I did the right thing and married your grandmother."

"You didn't love Nana?" Violet said, sounding one part sad and one part angry.

"Of course I did," Papa Ed responded with so much feeling that Lauren believed him. Plus, there was no way he could have feigned the obvious love for Nana Gloria all those years. "I cared for her before, but we had a fight about something stupid and inconsequential, and broke up. I started dating Verona and fell hard for her, but there was no way I was going to leave Gloria to raise our child alone. So we got married and moved away from Blue Falls."

"To get away from Verona?" Lauren asked.

"And to protect Gloria's reputation."

"But you still loved Verona?" Violet asked as she got up to pace the room.

Lauren didn't know how her sister found the energy to stand. She sure didn't have enough herself.

"Yes, but I never talked to her again." He hesitated, looking as if his mind had been transported to another time. "I didn't have the courage to face her, so I just left her a note telling her I had to go." He shook his head. "I handled it so wrong, but I was a scared kid who'd just found out he was going to be a father."

He sighed and shook his head slowly.

"Distance and time changed things," he said. "Gloria and I grew closer, and I would not trade all the years I had with her for anything. I loved her with all my heart." His voice broke on the last word.

Lauren reached over and took his hand in hers. "We know you did. That much was obvious."

"Is Verona the reason you wanted Lauren to come here, to open her restaurant in Blue Falls?" Violet was still pacing, in danger of wearing a visible path in the carpet.

Papa Ed shook his head. "No. I had no idea she was still here, or that she'd even recognize me if we did happen to cross paths. I just… I guess a part of me was homesick for my boyhood home after Gloria passed. I wanted to see it one more time. But when I happened across the empty restaurant for sale, it felt like some sort of sign. I can't really explain other than to say I thought..." He stopped and didn't appear as if he was going to go on.

It hit Lauren what he'd been about to say.

"You felt as if Nana was telling you something."

He nodded. "I know that sounds crazy, that I was just looking for a connection to her that wasn't there."

"I don't think it's crazy," Lauren said.

"You don't?" Violet looked at her sister as if she thought everyone in the room was off their rocker except for her and the sleeping babies.

"I think there are lots of things that none of us will ever fully understand. Whether Nana wanted us to come to Blue Falls, I have no idea. But I think the fact that Papa Ed ran into someone he used to love, someone who never got married, isn't pure coincidence."

"She never got married?" Papa Ed sounded shocked and as if maybe the news had broken his heart all over again.

"That's what I heard." She had to say something to banish the sadness she saw in his eyes. "But from all accounts she had a successful career and is now known far and wide as the town's unofficial matchmaker."

Lauren wondered if Verona spent so much time arranging happily-ever-afters for other people because she'd never gotten her own. The thought was incredibly sad, and there was just too damn much sadness in the world. Especially for good people.

"Maybe Nana wants you to have a second chance." Papa Ed's forehead crinkled in confusion.

"With Verona," Lauren said to clarify.

He shook his head. "Oh, no, I can't do that to her."

"Who? Nana or Verona?"

"I loved your grandmother."

Lauren squeezed his hand. "We know that. But you don't have to live the rest of your life alone to prove that to anyone, not even yourself."

"You're talking silliness," he said. "Besides, you saw how she reacted when she saw me. I doubt she ever wants to clap eyes on me again."

"You won't know until you ask."

"Lauren—"

It had been a long time since she'd shushed her little sister, but Lauren did it now. Violet looked shocked but thankfully kept quiet.

"I don't know." Papa Ed looked down at where Lauren's hand sat atop his.

"Listen, if nothing else maybe you can reconnect and set things right."

"It seems a little late for that."

"I'm speaking not as your granddaughter now, but as a woman. I saw the look on Verona's face. I don't really know her, but that look told me that she hasn't forgotten." Probably hadn't forgiven. "I think you have to try. If it doesn't work, then at least you tried. If you can be friends, even better. And if you can rekindle a spark, well, I want to see you happy. I've always worried about Mom being alone since Dad died, and I know you've been sad since Nana passed." Not to mention how she'd felt since the truth about Phil had come to light, though it wasn't the same thing. "It feels like time for our family to have something positive happen in the romantic realm, you know?"

"My money's on you," Papa Ed said as he looked up at her.

Lauren glanced at Violet, who shrugged. "I might have mentioned to Mom you were out on a date tonight."

"He seems like a fine young man, and the fact he took the girls with you speaks highly of him."

Papa Ed was likely using the turn in the conversation to avoid talking about Verona anymore, but Lauren had said her piece and any further action was up to him.

Time for her own honesty.

"He is. At least he seems to be."

Papa Ed sandwiched her hand between his. "We can never be one-hundred-percent certain about a person. We just have to go on our best judgment and faith."

"My belief in both of those is pretty shaky right now."

"But not shaky enough to prevent you from going back outside to grab a good-night kiss?" Violet asked, her natural teasing seeming to edge out her upset over Papa Ed's revelation.

"Did you leave the girls alone to spy on me?"

Violet smiled. "No, but you just confirmed my suspicion."

"We're not talking about me."

"Yeah, we are."

Lauren started to object before realizing she was just too tired.

Papa Ed stood. "I'll go and let you all get some rest. I feel as if I could sleep twelve hours myself."

Lauren accompanied him to the door. "Will you at least think about what I said?"

He placed his hand on her shoulder. "If you promise to give that young man a real chance. You deserve to be happy the same as the rest of us."

She nodded because she didn't know how else to respond. And the truth was those minutes in the parking lot had her thinking that she'd allowed herself to feel more for Adam than she'd even realized. If she was alone, she might very well close her eyes, touch her lips and relive every delicious moment of his kisses, the heart-pumping feel of his hands running over her. How much better would it feel if there was nothing between them?

Before her face lit up like a bright red railroad-crossing sign, she opened the door and kissed Papa Ed on the cheek. When she closed the door behind him, she halfway dreaded turning to face her sister. But the rest of her wanted to hop on her bed and tell Violet everything, to squeal like a teenage girl who'd just gone on a date with her dream guy.

Could Adam be that—a dream come true? Because the last man in her life had turned out to be a nightmare.

When she retraced her steps into the room, she found Violet sitting against the headboard of her bed.

"I honestly don't know what to even feel right now," Violet said.

"Papa Ed's not getting any younger. If there's the possibility that he could find love again, wouldn't you want him to?"

Violet shrugged. "I guess. But what if Verona hurts him instead? I don't want to have to go off on an old lady."

"I think Papa Ed can handle things himself." Not that she wouldn't be there for him if he needed it, but something was telling her that everything would be okay with him. Maybe Nana Gloria was speaking to her, too. She smiled at that thought.

"So, that smile have to do with what happened in

the parking lot? Speaking of, tell me exactly what did happen in the parking lot."

Lauren sat on the edge of her bed and flopped backward to stare at the ceiling. "Tell me I'm not being a fool."

"Well, I can't do that until you tell me what happened."

"I walked straight up to Adam and kissed him. Really kissed him."

"And did he kiss you back?"

"Yes."

"Peck? Smooch? French? I need details, woman."

Lauren lifted her feet. "Are there still soles on my shoes? Because it felt as if they might have melted off."

Violet squealed, causing one of the twins to make a startled sound in her sleep.

Lauren sat up straight and pointed at her sister. "If you wake them up, I'm going to leave you here with them and go sleep at the restaurant."

An evil grin spread across Violet's face. "Are you sure that's where you'd go? Or maybe you wouldn't be alone there."

Lauren's cheeks heated at the thought, at the way her skin tingled as if she could already feel Adam's hands there.

"My initial question remains."

"Are you a fool?" Violet scooted to the edge of her bed to face Lauren. "No. You'd be a fool if you let what happened with Phil keep you from finding happiness with someone else."

"But there are—"

Violet held up her hand. "I'm going to stop you right there. I understand why you do it—I probably would as well in your situation—but you need to stop overthinking everything. There is no way to know with total certainty that someone will never hurt you."

Lauren let out her breath and dropped her face into her hands for a few seconds before facing her sister again. "I really like him, but I'm scared. And it's not just me I have to consider now."

"The man just took your babies on a date with you."

"True."

"Go slowly if you want to, but just go."

Lauren bit her bottom lip and realized she could still taste Adam there. "Okay."

It took an amazing amount of willpower not to go immediately. Go toward what she hoped was the beginning of something great.

Chapter Thirteen

Adam smiled as he looked at the photo Lauren had just texted him. She was in the midst of cleaning out the flowerbeds around the restaurant building, thus hot, sweaty and dirty, with her hair escaping from the edges of the bandanna on her head.

Sure you still want to go out with this?

He typed a response.

More than ever.

She responded with several laughing emojis, but he was telling the truth. Since the night she'd walked out of the inn to kiss him two weeks before, they'd seen each other every day. And never missed an opportunity to kiss. Just the night before, she and her sister had come out to the ranch for dinner with the twins. He'd stolen Lauren away for a few minutes and taken her to the barn, where they had some time alone. Their kisses had gotten so hot and heavy that he'd had to force himself to step away. He wanted more, but he didn't know if she was ready to make herself that vulnerable, especially when he still saw doubt in her eyes sometimes. He counted himself lucky she'd gone as far as she had considering all he knew about Phil and how wrong he'd treated her. He hoped Phil was gone from her life for good, but he worried. The more he learned about the guy, the more he wondered if he'd really accept his humiliation without some sort of attempt at payback.

Phil had better not do anything that even approached hurting Lauren again. Or the twins. Adam had grown to love those little girls. It was impossible not to. And to say his mom had fallen for them too was the biggest of understatements. He knew without her saying a word that she was already envisioning them being her grandchildren someday.

Of course, that was putting the romantic cart way, way before the horse.

"That has to be the goofiest grin I've ever seen on your face, and that's saying something," Angel said as she plopped down on the opposite side of the dining room table, where he was sitting with his computer and a pile of paperwork he'd been working on before Lauren's text came in.

He placed his phone display down on the table. "Anyone ever tell you that you're a pest?"

"Repeatedly. It's the curse of being the baby of the family."

He scrolled down on his screen, making a notation about a new appointment he'd made a few minutes earlier to meet with a hotel owner in San Antonio. In order to increase the likelihood of making the branded-beef business profitable, he was expanding his area of exploration. He still hoped to be able to be Lauren's supplier, but lately business was the furthest thing from his mind when he was with her.

"So it seems things are going well with Lauren," Angel said.

"So far, so good."

Angel laughed.

He looked up from the computer screen. "What?"

"You've fallen for her."

He didn't deny it. He doubted there was any use.

"Have you told her?"

Adam shook his head. "I don't want to scare her away."

"You don't think she feels the same?"

He sat back in his chair with his hands laced behind his head. "I think she cares, but I could just be a re-bound relationship."

He hated the very thought of that being true because he fell for Lauren more each time they were together. Maybe he'd been falling since the first moment he'd met her and feared she'd topple off that rickety ladder.

"Not a chance."

Adam focused on his sister. "What makes you say that?"

"I'm a woman. I can tell when another woman more than just cares for a man. There's a difference between just wanting to get, shall we say, carnal with a guy and loving him."

"Okay, this conversation just got weird." Though the possibility that Lauren might be falling for him, too, sent a thrill through him he'd never experienced before.

Angel smiled. "I'm happy for you."

"Don't jinx it."

The fact that he worried something was going to

make Lauren change her mind kept dogging him over the next few days. When he was out meeting with clients, ironing out details with the meat packager, even when he was with Lauren. It didn't matter if they were sharing pizza at Gia's, helping his parents set up their enormous Christmas tree, or enjoying lingering kisses before they went their separate ways for the night, he couldn't shake the feeling that their time together was ticking down.

He told himself he was being paranoid, that he was just thinking that way because he wasn't sure how invested Lauren was in their relationship. Sure, she seemed to enjoy their time together. Really enjoy it when they were in each other's arms. But she hadn't even hinted she wanted more, and he was concerned if he pushed for it he'd lose her altogether. And she'd come to mean too much to him for her to not be in his life anymore.

He was getting ready to meet her for dinner at the Wildflower Inn when she texted that she'd moved to a cabin at the Vista Hills Guest Ranch and to meet her there and they'd figure out what to do for the evening.

She and Violet had talked about making the move as the twins got crankier with their teething, so maybe Lauren had finally decided to exchange the convenience of being in town for the privacy of being in a cabin, where the girls crying in the middle of the night wouldn't bother any other guests.

He waved at Ryan Teague as he passed him on the drive into the Teagues' guest ranch half an hour later. The family had done what he and his siblings hoped to—diversified their ranch's income to ensure its future survival.

When he reached the cabin Lauren had indicated, he noticed that only her car was parked next to it. Violet's and Ed's weren't anywhere in sight. The idea of actually being alone with Lauren sent a rush of heat through him.

As he walked up to the front door, he noticed the miniature Christmas tree that had been in their hotel room now sat on a table in the front window. He supposed he should start thinking about a Christmas present for Lauren. And something for the twins.

He raised his hand to knock on the door, but Lauren opened it before he could. She greeted him with a smile he had the sudden need to see every day for the rest of his life. Best not to say that out loud and risk freaking her out.

"You look beautiful," he said instead as he glanced at the bright blue dress that made her eyes look even bluer.

"Thanks." She ran her hand down the side of the dress, looking as if she was nervous.

That's when he noticed the candles and place settings on the dining table. *Two* place settings. His heart rate sped up. Then the delicious smells coming from the kitchen hit him and his stomach growled in response.

Lauren chuckled. "I hope that means you're hungry."

"You cooked?" Maybe that was why she'd moved to the cabin, so she'd have a kitchen again. Perhaps she had to do some cooking for her magazine pieces, or she was trying out new recipes for the restaurant.

"Yeah, I hope you don't mind that instead of going out."

Or maybe this was exactly what it looked like, a romantic dinner for two.

"Based on the smell, I doubt any place could beat it."

Adam stepped inside and shut the door against the December chill. He took Lauren's hand and gently pulled her close. "But I'd be happy eating gas-station food if it was with you."

He lowered his mouth to hers and indulged in a kiss that stoked the flames that had been smoldering within him since that night in the Wildflower Inn parking lot.

A ding from the kitchen caused Lauren to startle, thus ending the kiss.

"Sorry, I have to get that," she said before hurrying off toward the small kitchen area.

He watched as she bent to pull what looked and smelled like barbecued chicken from the oven.

"I know it's not beef, but this is one of my favorite dishes."

"I live on a cattle ranch. I can have beef anytime I want it."

A flash of something that almost looked like a wince crossed her face before she turned back to moving the casserole dish from the oven to the spot reserved for it on the table.

"Everything okay?"

"Yeah, fine."

But as they ate and talked about other things, he could tell something was still weighing on her mind. "Out with it," he said as he took her hand in his and ran his thumb across her knuckles.

"Nothing, just more annoyances at the restaurant this week. A variety of little things, but combined with the new roof and the unexpected wiring issues, I just sometimes wonder if I bit off more than I can chew."

"Nope. You're going to make this a big success, no doubt about it."

She stared at him as if looking for something more, then glanced down at where their hands were joined. "I need to tell you something."

Her tone concerned him, but the fact she'd made this delicious dinner just for the two of them indicated she wasn't going to toss him out of her life, right?

"Okay."

She looked up and it seemed she had a conflicting mix of determination and sorrow in her expression.

"I know you've been hoping to get a deal with the restaurant for your ranch's beef, but I promised myself that I would never again mix business with personal relationships. The last time I let the two coexist, it nearly destroyed my life."

Maybe he was wrong and she was about to dump him.

"I've loved all this time we've been spending together," she said. "I care about you, a lot, but if we continue to see each other, you have to know that I won't be able to use the Rocking Horse's beef."

He didn't realize until that moment how much he'd grown convinced that the deal was as good as signed, and a shot of anger went through him, as if he'd been strung along. But when he took a breath and considered everything she'd shared with him about what Phil had done, he had to admit he understood where she was coming from. A wave of concern about the viability of the branded-beef operation hit him, but he did his best to hide it. He'd figure out some way to make it profitable. He had to have faith something would present itself. The business had taken hits before and he always found some way to scrape by. But in that moment, the woman sitting across the table meant so much more to him than selling beef. He was pretty damn sure he loved her.

"If you think I'd walk away from you because of losing business, you're wrong." He lifted her hand and planted a soft kiss on her fingers without breaking eye contact.

She blinked eyes that looked brighter on the heels of his words. "How would you feel about skipping dessert?"

It took a moment for it to register what she meant. When it did, his entire body seemed to vibrate in anticipation. Instead of answering, he stood without releasing her hand and urged her to her feet. He pulled her close and caressed her cheek.

"Are you sure?"

"I won't lie and say I'm not nervous, but I've been fantasizing about this for a while."

He grinned. "That right?"

She ran her hand slowly up his chest. "Yes."

He glanced toward the clock on the mantel above the fireplace. "How long do we have?"

"All night."

Those flames within him exploded into a wildfire as he wrapped his arms around Lauren and captured her mouth with his.

LAUREN'S NERVOUSNESS ABOUT taking the next, huge step with Adam got shoved way into the background as he kissed her as if he was a hero in some great love story. She'd swear she heard a swell of romantic music wrap around them as she gave in to her desire. She kissed Adam back with the full force of all the feelings she'd been holding back for fear he'd crush her even more than Phil had.

Adam's hands on her bare arms made her want to rid them both of anything standing between more skin-on-skin contact. When had she ever felt so much potent desire? Ever?

She had loved Phil once, but she was certain the very idea of sex with him had never felt like what was consuming her now.

Not willing to wait any longer, she clasped Adam's hand and led him toward the bedroom. Once they were standing next to the bed, she slowly started to unbutton his shirt. He let her. His watching her without saying a word or making a move was the sexiest thing she'd ever experienced.

When she shoved his shirt from his arms and he simply let it drop to the floor, she had difficulty catching her breath. Unable to stop herself, she let her fingertips travel lightly over his exposed chest. His sharp intake of breath sent a thrill of power and excitement through her.

In the next moment he lowered his lips to hers again, and it seemed his hands were everywhere. So many places it was hard to focus. All her senses jumped from the taste of his lips and the feel of his tongue dueling with hers to the length of his body pressed against her to the slide of the zipper along the back of her dress.

Lauren wasn't a novice in the bedroom, but she'd never experienced anything like being undressed by Adam. He took his time even though she suspected there was a part of him that just wanted to rip off every stitch of their clothing and get to business. Or maybe that was just her.

Instead, he paused and ran his fingertips across the

swell of her breasts, kissed the curve of her shoulder, let his breath linger next to her ear, making her tingle from her scalp to the tips of her toes.

Needing to feel more of him, she ran her hands up his arms then pressed her lips against his chest. Feeling more daring than she ever had before, she ran her tongue along his warm flesh as her fingers began the work of freeing him from his jeans. The sharp intake of his breath was like a fresh supply of fuel to her desire.

Adam stepped out of his jeans and grabbed her at the back of her thighs, lifting her so that her legs were on either side of his hips as he crossed the rest of the distance to the bed. The strength it took for him to lower her slowly to the bed caused her pulse to accelerate.

"You're so beautiful," he said as he ran his fingertips along the edge of her face. The way he said those simple words made it apparent he believed what he said but that her physical attributes were not the only things that attracted him.

She wanted to tell him how handsome she thought he was, how being near him made her feel more alive than she ever had, but before she could speak he lowered his mouth to hers and she was lost.

What little was left of their clothing was tossed aside, leaving absolutely nothing between them. When Adam took care of the protection without her even having to ask, she fell for him even more. Not that she hated the idea of more children, especially with the right man, but at this stage she had all she could handle without losing her mind.

All of which she could tackle later. Now she wanted to focus on nothing but the man in her arms. And the feeling seemed to be mutual, judging by the way Adam was making every inch of her come alive beneath his touch.

The moment she'd been literally dreaming about arrived and she answered the question in his eyes with a smile. Everything else in her life disappeared as they made love. It wasn't just sex. And he wasn't only making love to her. It was the most beautiful give-and-take, like a ride on the world's most sensual roller coaster. When she felt herself approaching climax, she dug her fingers into Adam's strong shoulders, deriving even more pleasure from the feel of his muscles moving beneath his warm, taut skin.

She closed her eyes and pressed her head back into her pillow as she climaxed, followed in the next breath by Adam.

Her mind was still spinning when Adam curled around her body and pulled a quilt over them.

"Well, I don't need anything else for Christmas," he said.

She playfully swatted against his shoulder, causing him to laugh. Although she could safely echo his words and mean every one. So many things were flying through her mind, but she found herself drifting. Wasn't it the man who usually fell asleep approximately five seconds after finishing? Of course, between the various aspects of work and caring for two teething babies, sleep was a rare commodity. So feeling more relaxed than she had in ages, she snuggled close to Adam's warmth, smiling as he wrapped his wonderful arms around her, and allowed herself to drift toward blissful sleep.

IN THE DAYS following his night with Lauren, Adam alternated between whistling and grinning like a fool. At least that's how he felt. He'd never had a more wonderful night in his life, and the days since hadn't been half-bad either. He'd helped Lauren at the restaurant, and they were making decent progress despite minor annoyances continuing to crop up or how many times they got distracted by kissing and, well, other things.

Even business for the branded-beef operation was looking up. He'd signed a deal with a small restaurant in Fredericksburg, agreed to provide the steaks for a large society wedding in Austin, and was moments away from inking another contract to provide a variety of beef products for a newer winery bed-and-breakfast about an hour away from Blue Falls.

Jamie Barrett looked up before signing her portion of the agreement. "I know our customers are going to love your products."

"I appreciate your business."

"It's so exciting to think we'll have the same supplier as the Brazos Baker's new restaurant."

What? Where had she heard that?

"Maybe you can convince her to come out and do a demonstration for our guests sometime. And I'd love for her shop to carry some of our wine." The way she said it implied she knew that he and Lauren were dating and that he'd use his influence to give his customers special access.

Before he could correct her assumption, she signed her name on the contract with an excited flourish. Damn it. He'd have to tell Lauren about this and hope she didn't assume he'd used her the same way Phil had.

He could tell Jamie she was mistaken, but would that do more harm than good now? Though he'd not even mentioned Lauren, would Jamie feel misled into a business deal that wouldn't provide all the benefits she'd hoped? What if she decided to sue? Of course, she didn't have a case, but neither had Phil when he'd taken Lauren to court. Lauren had won but her business had taken a hit—the kind of hit his wouldn't survive. He'd just explain the situation to Lauren and ask her how she'd prefer he handle it. Maybe she'd even like the idea of working with the winery, despite how the connection had come about.

When he left a few minutes later, he sat in his truck staring at his phone. He didn't want to have this conversation with Lauren over the phone. He needed her to see his eyes when he told her, hear his voice in person. But that wouldn't be able to happen until later that night at the earliest. He had three more appointments, one of them all the way in Seguin, east of San Antonio. He'd been happy that his widening the area he was canvassing had yielded some results, but now he wondered if somehow word had gotten out that if someone did business with him they'd have an in with the famous Brazos Baker.

A sick pit formed in his stomach, not only at the potential mistake on everyone else's part, but also that his recent successes might have nothing to do with his hard work, or the quality of the Rocking Horse's beef.

Movement outside drew his attention and he looked up from where he'd been staring at his phone. Jamie gave him a big smile and a wave before she got into her car. Realizing he was going to be late to his next appointment if he didn't leave, he started the truck's engine and pulled out onto the road. But the sick, tight ball in his stomach didn't ease, not even when no one mentioned Lauren at his next meeting. Instead, it grew larger, and he remembered the feeling he'd had that something was going to derail his relationship with her.

Telling himself that he was simply blowing a misunderstanding out of proportion and promising himself he'd address it with Lauren as soon as he got back to Blue Falls, he drove toward his last appointment in Seguin even though he wanted nothing more than to race back home to Lauren. But he needed to keep building his business, to succeed on his own so that no one, not even Lauren, could say he'd only succeeded because of his association with her. To prove to her that he didn't need or want part of her company. He only wanted her.

Chapter Fourteen

Lauren paused outside of the Blue Falls Tourist Bureau and Chamber of Commerce's combined office when she got a text. She smiled when she saw it was from Adam. Just the thought of him made her happier than she'd ever been. The time they spent together was the most awesome reward for her allowing herself to believe she might find love again, and with someone who wouldn't betray her.

Can I see you when I get back to town later?

Of course the answer was yes, no matter how tired she was at the end of a long day. She typed her response.

Yes. What time will you be back?

In two or three hours. Last meeting got delayed.

Okay, heading into the business holiday mixer.

Have a good time.

She'd have a better time with him, but she needed to push those sexy thoughts aside so that no one could read them on her face like a headline in two-hundred-point bold type. When she stepped inside, she spotted her sister. Papa Ed was on babysitting duty tonight along with Verona, who had finally warmed up to him after they'd had several long talks about the past and the intervening years over coffee and pastries.

"From the grin on your face, you must have just talked to a certain hunky cowboy," Violet said.

"Possibly."

Lauren glanced around the room filled with people who owned businesses in Blue Falls and the surrounding Hill Country. This was a social event for the holidays, but she was hoping to make more connections now that the time to actually start planning for the restaurant's opening was near. Earlier that day, she'd met with some food vendors, and a couple of days before, she and Adam had driven the arts-and-crafts trail so she could meet local artisans. She came away with plans to carry some of their items in her gift shop.

Though he didn't say anything, she suspected that Adam wished there was a way for them to be together and still have the Rocking Horse's beef served in her restaurant. Honestly, she'd been thinking about caving. After all, Adam was nothing like Phil. And what were the odds that two men in a row would use her success to advance their own? Could she mix business with pleasure again?

She and Violet began to mingle as they snacked on a variety of yummy hors d'oeuvres. It wasn't until Lauren bit into a crab-stuffed mushroom that she realized how hungry she was, that she'd barely eaten all day with how packed her schedule had been. Between meeting with vendors and overseeing the polishing of the floor, not to mention doing some editing on her next cookbook, lunch had come and gone with her only managing to down a leftover mini pork slider from the night before.

A pretty redhead wearing a wide smile approached Lauren just as she swallowed the last bite of mushroom. The other woman extended her hand.

"Lauren Shayne, it's so nice to meet you," she said. "Jamie Barrett. I own a winery and bed-and-breakfast about a half hour on the other side of Poppy."

Lauren shook the other woman's hand. "Nice to meet you, too."

"I'm sure you hear this a lot, but I'm a big fan. I was just telling Adam that this afternoon when we finalized our deal to serve Rocking Horse beef. I figure if it's good enough for the Brazos Baker, it's a 'can't lose' business decision on my part."

The appetizers she'd eaten threatened to come back up. Surely this woman wasn't saying what it sounded like, that Adam was telling potential customers that she'd agreed to serve Rocking Horse Ranch beef in her restaurant. That couldn't be right. He'd chosen her over business. Hadn't he? She had to know the truth, but the moment she opened her mouth to ask for clarification, Violet was suddenly at her elbow.

"I'm sorry to interrupt, but do you mind if I borrow my sister for a minute?" Violet asked Jamie.

"Not at all. The night's young. Maybe we can chat about your gift shop carrying a selection of our wine later."

Violet made a noncommittal sound and practically dragged Lauren out to the building's lobby.

"I know what you're thinking, and I don't want you

to jump to conclusions," Violet said before Lauren could object to her sister's behavior.

"What else could it mean?" Her stomach started to churn. "Oh, my God, I've been a complete fool yet again."

"No, you haven't."

"You don't know that." Lauren pointed toward the gathering in the other part of the building. "Because it sounded a whole lot like Adam told that woman that we would be serving Rocking Horse beef at the restaurant when we're not."

"It could just be a misunderstanding."

"How? How could there be a misunderstanding if the topic doesn't even come up? And if it did, why didn't he correct her?"

"I don't know, but perhaps that's something you should ask him."

Lauren forced herself to take a deep breath, to try not to jump to the most-dreaded conclusion. After all, she'd even given Phil the benefit of the doubt until she'd had irrevocable proof that he'd betrayed her, used her. The mere thought that Adam might have done the same, knowing how much it had hurt her the last time, made her heart ache terribly.

"Adam isn't like Phil," Violet said.

"You don't know that for sure."

"I'd bet every cent I have that I'm right. You're letting your old fears shove aside how great these past weeks have been for you. I haven't seen you this happy in a very long time." Violet made a dismissive motion with her hand. "No, I take that back. I've never seen you this happy. Adam is a good guy, and he's good for you.

He deserves a chance to explain, if he's even aware of what's going on."

Lauren wanted to believe her sister, to believe in Adam's faithfulness, but she couldn't silence the doubts barraging her mind. If he had betrayed her, she was done with men. She would follow in her mother's footsteps and raise her daughters alone, live the rest of her life surrounded only by the family she already had and be content with that.

But as she thought about life without Adam in it, tears welled in her eyes.

"Let's go back inside and mingle some more," Violet said. "I was just talking to Ryan Teague and I love the idea of carrying his carved wooden angels in the shop."

Lauren shook her head. "I can't. You go ahead, but I'm going back to the restaurant."

"You've already put in, what, twelve hours today?"

"I aim to talk to Adam about this tonight, and I'd rather do it somewhere other than the cabin." If this ended up being the end of her and Adam, she didn't want to have the rest of her family witness the demise of yet another of her relationships.

Violet grabbed Lauren's hands. "Please just give him a chance to explain, and try to listen without having already judged him guilty."

Lauren nodded. "I will."

Because she would love nothing more than for Jamie Barrett to have made the entire thing up, though that didn't seem likely, either.

"Want me to go with you? I can stay until he gets there."

"No. I'd rather have some time to think and calm down by myself."

"Okay, but I'm only a call or text away. The beauty of small towns—I can be there in a handful of minutes."

Lauren bit her lip as she accepted a hug from Violet before heading out to her car and driving back to the restaurant. Every conversation, every interaction she'd ever had with Adam, replayed in her head. She hoped the fact that she couldn't think of anything that made him look guilty was a good sign, but she remembered she hadn't suspected Phil, either.

Unbidden, reasons why Adam might betray her in the same way bubbled up from the darkest part of her mind. He wanted to increase his own business, which he'd admitted had been hard, by association with someone more successful. He was upset that she had refused to do business with him. Did he think that if it got out that she would be serving Rocking Horse beef, she'd have to reverse her decision? Heck, even the building she'd bought had once been part of his big plan for the Rocking Horse's future.

But he'd told her he understood why she couldn't buy his products and have a romantic relationship with him at the same time. And she'd believed him. Had he done so knowing he could benefit from their relationship in another way?

She pulled into the parking lot outside the restaurant but didn't immediately get out of her car. She felt as if any strength or energy she'd once possessed had been siphoned out of her the moment Jamie Barrett had introduced herself. But sitting here in the dark wasn't going to accomplish anything. If she was going to stay here and wait for Adam's return, she could at least get some more work done. There were dishes to order and menus to plan and a sign to design. Violet had worked on a lot of those things earlier, but it was still Lauren's job to finalize every aspect of her business.

She drew a shaky breath, almost as if her lungs had forgotten how to work in concert, and headed inside. Suddenly, she got the feeling someone was watching her—the same as that night at the inn. A chill ran down her spine as she remembered the two drunk guys outside the music hall. Did they blame her for their arrest? Had they come back and found her even more alone this time? She hurried toward the building since it was closer than her car.

As soon as she stepped through the door and her foot made a splashing sound, the creeped-out feeling gave way to a hard thud of her heart against her chest.

Oh, no. No, no, no!

She flicked on the overhead lights to reveal the awful truth. As far as she could see in each direction, the floor stood under what looked like an indoor lake.

WHEN ADAM RETURNED to Blue Falls and texted Lauren, she didn't respond with where he could find her. He noticed several people standing around talking outside the tourist bureau office, so he parked and went in search of her. Maybe she'd gotten to chatting with other business owners and hadn't heard her phone.

"Hey, Adam," Keri Teague said when she spotted him. "You missed the festivities."

"I'm looking for Lauren. She said she was here earlier."

A concerned expression erased Keri's smile. "She left pretty early in the evening. Then Violet left soon thereafter, rather quickly."

There was no way they could have found out about

the misunderstanding with Jamie Barrett, was there? Did Lauren just have a sixth sense for betrayal now and had somehow detected it without him saying a word?

A couple of the other people standing outside moved to leave, and what he saw made his heart stop. Jamie Barrett stood talking with India Parrish, owner of Yesterwear Boutique. Without saying goodbye to Keri, he strode straight toward the other woman.

"Excuse me," he said, butting in to the conversation between Jamie and India, then staring straight at Jamie. "Can I speak with you?"

He knew he sounded abrupt, but this was partly— no, there was no *partly* about it. This was *entirely* his fault, but he had to know if what he was assuming was indeed true.

India, likely detecting his mood, moved away after saying it was nice to chat with Jamie.

"Is something wrong?" Jamie looked so genuinely concerned that he did his best to calm down.

"Did you talk to Lauren here tonight?"

Jamie smiled. "Oh, yes. Such a lovely person. I might have gushed a bit about being a fan."

He bit his bottom lip before asking his next question. "Did you mention our business deal?"

Now she appeared confused. "Yes. Why?"

He took a fortifying breath, knowing what he was about to say might lead to the invalidation of his contract with her and quite possibly send a ripple of bad publicity out about Rocking Horse Ranch. Might even sound the death knell for the branded-beef business. He'd deal with that if the time came. Making things right with Lauren was more important.

"I allowed you to believe that Lauren's restaurant

would be serving our beef products, but it won't be. We decided to keep our personal and professional relationships separate. I'm sorry about the misunderstanding, and I'll understand if you want to cancel our contract."

"Oh, my God," Jamie said with a gasp. "Please tell me I didn't mess up things between you."

Adam hadn't expected that reaction and it took him a few seconds to form an appropriate reply. "I don't know. I'm sure it'll be okay."

He sure hoped so.

"I'm so sorry."

"It's not your fault. It's mine. If you'll excuse me…"

He had to find Lauren. Before driving all the way out to the Vista Hills Guest Ranch, he headed toward the restaurant. Chances were better than average that she was there, considering how much time she spent working toward her goal of being open before the spring wildflowers started blooming.

When he pulled into the parking lot, he noticed not only Lauren's vehicle, but also Violet's. And the front door was standing wide open. He'd much rather talk to Lauren by herself, but he couldn't put off the conversation even if Violet was within earshot.

He heard the slosh of water as he approached the entrance before it registered why. He stopped at the threshold and just stared at the water covering every inch of the floor. Lauren looked up at him from where she stood in the middle of it with her sister.

"What happened?"

"I need to know you didn't do this," Lauren said, looking as if she were on the verge of breaking down. "And don't lie."

Shocked by the question and the heat of the anger toward him, he just stared at her for a long moment. "Of course not. Why would I do this?"

"Revenge."

A wave of his own anger rose up so fast that it nearly choked Adam. Yes, he'd made a mistake not correcting Jamie's assumption immediately, but how could Lauren think he'd do this kind of damage to her restaurant? It made no sense, and he didn't deserve her anger—at least not for that. Especially when he'd been nothing but supportive despite the fact she refused to do business with his family's ranch.

Before he could vent his anger, Violet stepped forward. "She's upset. Someone came in and deliberately flooded the place by turning on every faucet, the water heater and just about every water valve in the building, not to mention stopping up the sinks and toilets."

"Phil," he growled. Who else would have this much obvious hate for Lauren?

"That's my thought." Violet looked over her shoulder toward Lauren. "But she's upset and doubting—"

"Because of Jamie Barrett."

Violet looked startled for a moment before nodding. "I'll wait outside while you two talk."

Despite how frustrated and mad he was, Adam wanted to hug Violet. She seemed to believe in him despite everything that potentially put him in the same horrible light as Lauren's ex-fiancé. She gave his upper arm a quick squeeze of support before heading outside.

He cringed at the sound his feet made moving through the water, and he shivered. December was far from the best month for something like this to happen, if there was such a thing. Thank goodness they weren't somewhere like Montana.

"You should get out of the water before you catch a chill." He might be upset by her attack, but he still cared about her.

"I doubt I could get any colder."

He didn't think she was talking entirely about the water and the winter air.

"I stopped by the tourist bureau and I saw Jamie Barrett—"

"Did you use me, Adam?"

"No." The answer came out fast and sharp, with the same kind of edge as her accusatory questions. "I didn't even know she had any idea we knew each other until she mentioned it right as she was signing the contract." He stepped toward her and brought his hands up to touch her, but she moved away as if she never wanted to touch him again. "I swear to you on my life that I would never treat you the way Phil did."

He told her every single detail of the meeting, including how he'd been so surprised by the turn in the conversation that he'd made the mistake of not immediately correcting Jamie's erroneous assumption. She listened but the way she held herself stiff, arms wrapped around herself, made him wonder if his words were getting through.

"It's what I wanted to talk to you about when I texted you earlier, but I wanted to tell you in person."

He couldn't tell if she believed him, and he grudgingly admitted that from her point of view it could be seen as a convenient explanation.

"It doesn't matter now," she said.

"What do you mean?"

She gestured toward the standing water. "It's the final straw, a sign that this wasn't meant to be."

Adam feared she was talking about more than the restaurant.

"You're insured, right?"

"Yes, but I'm just tired." And she sounded it. Below the anger and perceived betrayal, she sounded completely spent. "I put so much into this place even though it was crazy to start a business so far from where I live. There were all the unexpected expenses. I need to just stick to what I know and chalk this up to another of my huge life mistakes."

He got the feeling she was lumping her relationship with him into that mistake. Still, he wanted to pull her close, make her believe that she could get through this and have success on the other side. But instinct told him that she wouldn't be receptive to any of that. And a part of him was ticked off that she was pushing him away, using this setback as an excuse to put her walls back up. But he clamped down on that part that wanted to scream at her to stop feeling sorry for herself and see the truth.

"You need a hot shower and a good night's sleep. Tomorrow is soon enough to deal with this."

"I can't leave yet. I'm waiting for the sheriff."

His heart thumped, but then he realized why Simon Teague would be called. If it was obvious someone had sabotaged the restaurant, this was a crime scene.

The arrival of another vehicle outside, followed by a second, proved to be Simon and one of his deputies, Conner Murphy, who'd just gotten free of another call on the far side of the county. Over the next hour, the two questioned Lauren, Violet and Adam. He'd had to account for his whereabouts from the time Lauren left the restaurant until she'd returned to find the flooding. Even though Adam hadn't had anything to do with the damage, he found himself squirming and forcing himself to keep a lid on his frustration when Lauren wouldn't even look at him.

By the time all statements were taken and what felt like thousands of photos snapped of the damage and the identified sources, it was getting late and Lauren looked as if she might fall over from exhaustion. To be honest, he was beginning to feel the same. He wanted nothing more than for Lauren to realize she'd been wrong to suspect him so he could curl up with her, comfort her and sleep until noon the next day. But the fact that she couldn't meet his eyes told him she wouldn't welcome the company. He just needed to give her time to rest and come to grips with the shock of what had happened. Hopefully, then she'd be able to forgive him for his mistake and believe he'd never deliberately betray her.

As they all walked outside, Lauren paused next to her car as if feeling she needed to say something, but either didn't know what or didn't have the energy.

"You look completely exhausted," he said. "I don't think you should drive right now."

"She won't," Violet said as she approached them.

Violet may very well believe he was innocent in the vandalism, but she was wearing enough protective-sister vibes that he took a step away from Lauren.

"I'll call you tomorrow," he said to Lauren.

After Violet got into the driver's seat and started the car, Lauren turned halfway toward him but still didn't look him in the eye.

"Please don't." She took a shaky breath. "I can't do this."

His heart sank. "Do what?"

"I can't be with someone I can't trust."

"I didn't do this. You know that."

She motioned between the two of them. "This was a mistake."

Damn it, he was getting angry again. "You're using your past as an excuse to run away. That's not fair, to either of us."

"Life's not fair."

Her complete belief in her words, that life had once again put someone in her path who'd betrayed her, hollowed him out as he watched her get into the car and close the door. As he watched the Shayne sisters drive away into the night, the night seemed to cry out that it was for the last time.

Chapter Fifteen

Adam listened to the laughter of his family in the living room as they opened up a round of Christmas gag gifts. He'd somehow made it through the big holiday meal and the opening of his gifts before he vacated the room. There were few times in his life he'd felt less like celebrating.

He sat on the side of his bed turning the small, gift-wrapped box in his hands over and over. He'd looked forward to giving the silver charm bracelet to Lauren, imagined her smiling as she examined the tiny spatula, mixing bowl, whisk and cookbook. He should have returned it for a refund by now because it was obvious they were over. He didn't know it was possible for a person to feel this empty.

She'd been gone for a week without a word. Even his anger couldn't cover up his heartache anymore.

Someone knocked on his bedroom door and he shoved the box into a drawer in his dresser.

"Yeah."

Angel opened the door then came to sit beside him on the bed. "Missing Lauren, huh?"

He nodded. No sense in pretending otherwise.

"Have you talked to her?"

"No." Some of his anger tried to reassert itself when he thought about how his voice mails and texts had been met with telling silence.

"You're not giving up, are you?"

"She doesn't want anything to do with me, and I don't want to be with someone who looks at me and only sees the ways I might betray her."

"Maybe she just needs time to get over the shock of what happened."

He shook his head. "She's not coming back to Blue Falls."

"Then you need to make sure she has a reason to come back."

He sighed. "Such as?"

"Well, you could start by telling her you love her, for one."

He didn't even bother asking Angel how she knew that when he'd just admitted the truth to himself in the days since Lauren had left town.

"Pretty sure she wouldn't believe me." And did he even want to admit the truth to a woman who'd so easily dumped him?

"Won't know until you try. And remember what we told Ben when he was trying to win Mandy—women love big, romantic gestures."

He was lying in bed later that night thinking about what his sister had said. A big, romantic gesture. Was he willing to try one more time to save what he and Lauren had? Could he think of something that would fit that "big, romantic gesture" description? He fell asleep still turning the idea over and over in his head, but it wasn't until he woke up the next morning that the perfect plan came to him. At least he hoped it was perfect. But he couldn't do it alone.

"Where are you headed?" Angel asked when he was walking out the front door with his truck keys a while later.

"Operation Big, Romantic Gesture."

Angel pumped her fist. "Yes!"

Adam laughed for the first time in more than a week.

LAUREN TESTED THE lemon cake she'd just baked and found it lacking. She shoved it across the counter in frustration.

"What's wrong?" Violet asked as she entered their kitchen.

"I've lost my ability to bake anything remotely edible."

Violet came over and took a bite. "Are you kidding? This is delicious."

"You're just saying that." Her entire family had been noticeably careful around her since their return home.

"When have I ever given you false praise?"

Admittedly that wasn't her sister's style.

"Okay, enough," Violet said. "You're finding fault with your baking because you're not willing to admit you screwed up with Adam."

Lauren wanted to defend herself but it was difficult to find the words. Maybe because she knew Violet was right. Even before she'd found out that Phil was behind the flooding, the rock through the window and even the creepy feelings of being watched, she'd realized she'd been wrong to doubt Adam.

Lauren stared out the window at the Brazos River.

"I've let too much time pass. He'll never be able to forgive me."

"Think maybe you're underestimating him again?"

Was she? "How do I fix this?"

"I suggest groveling. And, oh, I don't know, telling him the truth."

Violet's suggestions were a good start, but she needed something more, something bigger.

It wasn't until she was walking beside the river later and spotted her neighbor's cattle that the answer came to her. She smiled then hurried back to the house.

Violet and the twins startled when Lauren came rushing back in.

"What in the world is chasing you?"

"A plan to win back Adam."

"Which is?"

"Cows."

Violet looked at the girls. "Your mom has gone crazy."

Yeah, crazy in love.

LAUREN WATCHED THE world flash by outside the passenger-side window of Violet's car. It'd been almost three weeks since she'd been in Blue Falls, and her stomach was in knots as they got closer. What if she'd totally ruined her chances with Adam? What if the fact she was asking for his forgiveness only after the investigation cleared him made him believe she'd never trust him? She'd been missing Adam terribly. But after she'd run away from him after basically accusing him of being just like Phil and then not communicating with him, she couldn't imagine that he'd welcome the sight of her. She had to change his mind.

At least Papa Ed's romantic prospects were looking up. He and Verona were taking it slowly, but they talked every day and had discovered the spark that had once burned between them was still there. Older, wiser, but still there.

Violet pulled over at a gas station at the edge of Blue Falls. "Gotta pee."

"We're literally a mile from the restaurant." Where her grand plan had to be put into motion.

"When you've got to go, you've got to go."

Violet thankfully didn't take long. When they reached the restaurant, Lauren felt a wave of exhaustion similar to the night she'd left here. The thought of all the work she faced could overwhelm her if she let it. But right now that took a back seat to winning back the man she loved.

"Ready to go in?" Violet asked.

She nodded.

"We should probably see how things look before we take that in." Violet pointed over her shoulder toward Lauren's gift to Adam.

"Agreed." She didn't want to lug it inside only to find the water removal and mold remediation hadn't worked.

Violet walked in ahead of Lauren then quickly stepped to the side.

"Surprise!"

Lauren jumped at the sound of so many voices calling out at once. At first her mind couldn't comprehend what she was seeing, but then she started to recognize individual faces. Her mother and Papa Ed holding the twins. Verona smiling as she gripped Papa Ed's arm. Several of the town's other business owners. Even Jamie

Barrett. And the entirety of the Hartley family stood smiling at Lauren.

Her heart leaped when she spotted Adam standing right in the middle.

They all stood on a brand-new floor. The tables and chairs she'd ordered were set up, ready for diners. Art hung on the walls. The corner devoted to the gift shop was prepped to receive merchandise.

"I don't understand," she said, her words having to push their way past the lump in her throat.

"Adam organized the community to fix what Phil tried to destroy," Violet said.

Lauren couldn't hold back the tears anymore. "I can't believe what you all did here."

"We weren't going to let your dream die," Papa Ed said. "Adam is one determined young man."

"Thank you." The words felt so weak, so unable to convey the depth of her gratitude. Nowhere near powerful enough to let this man know how much he meant to her. She hoped the work he'd put into resurrecting her restaurant meant he could forgive her, that this wasn't just a grand apology for the misunderstanding with Jamie Barrett.

The crowd moved then, some coming forward to greet her and say how excited they were about the restaurant's future opening and others moving toward a wide assortment of food. She eventually made her way through all the well-wishers to Adam. She faced him with her heart threatening to beat so fast she couldn't distinguish between one beat and the next.

"I can't believe you did this," she said.

"I had a lot of help."

"It looks beautiful. I don't know how I'll ever be able to thank you."

"If you'll give us another chance, that's enough."

She bit her lip to keep it from trembling before responding. "I was thinking on the way here how you'd never be able to forgive me. I'm sorry for how I doubted you, how I ran away and broke off all contact."

Adam stepped forward and placed his palms gently against her shoulders. "Part of me understood."

"But part didn't."

"It hurt that you could believe I'd do anything to harm you, but I've let that go."

"Why?" He had every right to be upset.

"Because I'm hopelessly in love with you."

Her lip trembled. "I love you, too."

Adam's eyes widened as if he hadn't expected his feelings to be reciprocated. "Can I kiss you?"

"I wish you would."

His lips had barely touched hers when she heard applause. Adam's mouth curved into a smile for just a moment before he pulled her close and sealed his declaration with a kiss that erased any last vestiges of doubt that might have been hanging around in her mind, waiting to pounce.

Over the next hour or so, she enjoyed spending time with the people that she now knew were the very best kind of friends. When everyone finally left, leaving her and Adam alone, he escorted her out to the stone patio that would be used for outdoor dining come spring.

"I have something I want to give you," he said as he produced a small box wrapped in red foil.

"You've already given me the best gift possible." And she didn't just mean the repairs to the restaurant.

"This was your Christmas present I wasn't able to give you."

She accepted the box and opened it. When she saw the silver charm bracelet, she ran her fingertip over the adorable charms. "It's perfect."

"I'm glad you like it."

"I have a present for you, too."

"Another kiss, I hope."

She didn't argue with that assumption and kissed him, trying to make up for the time they'd been apart.

"While very enjoyable," she said when they finally parted, "that wasn't what I was going to say. You weren't the only one who had plans of trying to get back together today."

"Well, now I'm really curious."

She nodded toward the gift she'd had Violet and her mom hide out here.

"What is it?"

"Uncover it and find out."

He lifted the blanket to reveal a sign she'd had made—Brazos Baker Gift Shop, Featuring the Rocking Horse Ranch Collection.

"And when Brazos Baker Barbecue opens in the spring, we're going to be serving Rocking Horse Ranch beef."

He stared down at her as if he didn't trust what he'd seen or heard. "What happened to not mixing business with personal relationships?"

"I thought I needed that policy in place to protect me from making another stupid mistake." She lifted her hand to his face and smiled. "I don't need it anymore because letting myself love you was the best decision I've ever made."

"You're not scared?"

"Not one bit." She waited for the inner fear she'd carried around for so long to make a liar of her, but it didn't appear. She was pretty sure it no longer existed.

"Does this mean you might move to Blue Falls?"

She let her hands slide down the front of his shirt. "You might be able to convince me."

Adam pulled her close to his delicious, strong warmth and set about convincing. She'd already made her decision that Blue Falls would be her new home, but maybe she'd let him think she needed convincing for a little bit longer.

"You've already decided, haven't you?" he asked.

"Yes. But that doesn't mean we have to stop this."

He grinned. "You're right, it doesn't."

And his lips returned to hers.

* * * * *

If you loved this novel, don't miss Trish Milburn's other BLUE FALLS, TEXAS *books:*

A RANCHER TO LOVE
THE COWBOY TAKES A WIFE
IN THE RANCHER'S ARMS

And more, available now at Harlequin.com!

We hope you enjoyed this story from
Harlequin® Western Romance.

Harlequin® Western Romance is coming to an end, but community, cowboys and true love are here to stay. Starting July 2018, discover more heartfelt tales of family and friendship from **Harlequin® Special Edition**.

Romance is for life, and these stories show that every chapter in a relationship has its challenges and delights and that love can be renewed with each turn of the page!

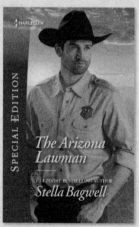

Look for six *new* romances every month
from **Harlequin® Special Edition!**
Available wherever books are sold.

Western Romance

Available April 3, 2018

#1685 THE TEXAS COWBOY'S BABY RESCUE
Texas Legends: The McCabes
by Cathy Gillen Thacker

When nurse Bridgett Monroe finds an abandoned newborn baby, everyone thinks Cullen Reid McCabe is the father. But this honest cowboy is determined to find the child's real family—with Bridgett's help.

#1686 COWBOY SEAL DADDY
Cowboy SEALs • by Laura Marie Altom

Paisley Carter has been burned by love, but pregnancy hormones have her crushing on her sexy SEAL pretend fiancé! Then a weekend on Wayne's ranch has Paisley thinking she and Wayne should unite for real.

#1687 REUNITED WITH THE BULL RIDER
Gold Buckle Cowboys • by Christine Wenger

Callie Wainwright romanced cowboy Reed Beaumont in their youth, but his burgeoning career as a bull rider called a halt to their happily-ever-after. But the boy is back in town, and the sparks between them are as hot as ever.

#1688 THE COWBOY'S SURPRISE BABY
Spring Valley, Texas • by Ali Olson

Amy McNeal broke Jack Stuart's heart back in high school. Now she's pregnant, and they have to get over their painful past and try to be a family—for the baby's sake.

Get 2 Free Books,
Plus 2 Free Gifts—
just for trying the Reader Service!

HARLEQUIN® SPECIAL EDITION

HSE17R3

Could Bridgett Monroe's shocking discovery soften the notoriously rigid Cullen McCabe?

Read on for a sneak preview of
THE TEXAS COWBOY'S BABY RESCUE,
the first book in Cathy Gillen Thacker's series
TEXAS LEGENDS: THE MCCABES.

Cullen McCabe slammed to a halt just short of her.

His dark brows lowered like thunderclouds over mesmerizing blue eyes. Her breath caught in her chest.

"Is this an April Fool's joke?" he demanded gruffly.

Suddenly feeling angry, Bridgett gestured at the sleeping infant beyond the nursery's glass window. The adorable newborn had curly espresso brown hair and gorgeous blue eyes.

Just like the man in front of her.

"Does this look like a joke, McCabe?" Because it sure wasn't to Bridgett, who'd found the abandoned baby.

Their eyes clashed, held for an interminably long moment. Cullen looked back, lingering on the tag attached to the infant bed: Robby Reid McCabe.

"What do I have to do with this baby? Other than that we apparently share the same last name?"

Bridgett reached into the pocket of her scrubs and withdrew the rumpled envelope. "This was left beside the fire station along with the child."

With a scowl, he opened the envelope, pulled out the typewritten paper and read out loud, "Cullen, I know you never planned to have a family or get married, and I understand that, but please be the daddy little Robby deserves."

Reacting like he'd landed on some crazy reality TV show, Cullen looked around suspiciously.

To no avail. The only cameras were the security ones the hospital employed. As Cullen stepped closer to the glass and gave the baby another intent look, Bridgett inched nearer and stared up at him. At six foot four, he towered over her.

"You found him?"

She nodded.

Cullen's expression radiated compassion. "I'm sorry to hear that." His voice dropped. "But unfortunately, I don't have any connection to this baby."

"Sure about that?"

He frowned at her. "Think I'd know if I'd conceived a child with someone."

"Not necessarily," she countered. Not if he hadn't been told.

Briefly, a deep resentment seemed to flicker in his gaze.

He lowered his face to hers and spoke in a masculine tone that sent a thrill down her spine. "I'd know if I'd slept with someone in the last ten months or so."

He paused to let that sink in. "Obviously, you don't believe me."

Bridgett shrugged. "It's not up to me to believe you or not." This was becoming too personal, too fast.

*Don't miss THE TEXAS COWBOY'S BABY RESCUE
by Cathy Gillen Thacker, available April 2018
wherever Harlequin® Western Romance books
and ebooks are sold.*

www.Harlequin.com